hard sell

OTHER TITLES BY LAUREN LAYNE

21 Wall Street Series

Hot Asset

I Do, I Don't

Ready to Run

Runaway Groom

Stiletto and Oxford

After the Kiss

Love the One You're With

Just One Night

The Trouble with Love

Irresistibly Yours

I Wish You Were Mine

Someone Like You

I Knew You Were Trouble

I Think I Love You

Love Unexpectedly (stand-alone novels)

Blurred Lines

Good Girl

Love Story

Walk of Shame

An Ex for Christmas

The Wedding Belles

From This Day Forward (novella)

To Have and to Hold

For Better or Worse

To Love and to Cherish

New York's Finest

Frisk Me

Steal Me

Cuff Me

Redemption

Isn't She Lovely

Broken

Crushed

The Best Mistake

Only with You

Made for You

hard sell

LAUREN LAYNE

Published by Montlake Romance, Seattle

www.apub.com

ISBN-13: 9781503902848
ISBN-10: 1503902846

Cover design by Letitia Hasser

Printed in the United States of America

For Anth—
for letting me get especially lost in the writer-zone
on this book,
and for making sure my coffee cup was never empty

1

Matt

Monday Morning, September 18

"You're an angel, and I love you," I say with a reverence usually reserved for people in church.

My assistant lifts an eyebrow and holds out two aspirin. "Are you talking to me or the bagel sandwich?"

"Both," I say around a bite, holding out my free hand for the pills.

Kate waits until I swallow, then holds out a Venti Starbucks cup that I use to wash down the pills.

"How'd you know?" I ask, picking up the egg and Swiss on sesame bagel once more.

"That you were hungover as crap? I get your flight change notifications. Taking an unplanned Sunday red-eye from Vegas to New York after a bachelor party pretty much says it all."

I wince. "Can we not say the word *Vegas*? Or *bachelor party*? And until further notice, all references to alcohol are hereby banned."

She smirks. "It sucks getting old, huh?"

"I'm not old," I say automatically. The very suggestion's an affront. After all, I'm Matt Cannon, Wall Street's legendary wunderkind.

And yeah, only douchebags would call themselves legendary, but in my case? It's kind of true. I graduated from high school when I was sixteen, college when I was nineteen, and got hired on at Wolfe Investments just days after my twenty-second birthday, back when my liver was basically a virgin (though I was *definitely* not) and more than ready to take on the booze-fest that is Wall Street.

Whoops. I just remembered we're not talking about alcohol. Not until the aspirin, caffeine, and this sandwich work their sweet magic on my hangover.

Anyway, the point is I'm only twenty-eight. Not exactly a boy wonder anymore, but to be one of the Wolfes before thirty is brag-worthy. It's hard enough to get hired by the company in the first place, even harder to move up the ranks at such a young age, and . . .

Oh hell, who am I kidding?

I can't drink like I could when I was twenty-two, and I am officially feeling the effects of the forty-eight-hour rager that was my cousin's bachelor party.

"How are you feeling, for real?" Kate asks, giving me a critical once-over.

Kate Henley's one of those assistants who you guard more closely than your wallet, Pappy Van Winkle, or bank account password. She's that valuable.

Sure, she's got the petite, pretty, doe-eyed look of a 1950s debutante, but she's obscenely competent at her job. So competent, in fact, she works for not one demanding boss but *three*. A couple of years ago, I got promoted to director the same month as my two best friends and Wolfe colleagues, Ian Bradley and Kennedy Dawson. The promotion meant we each got our own assistant instead of sharing one like the junior guys. We couldn't decide who got Kate, so she took on all three of us and does it twice as well as any of the other assistants who support only one investment broker.

Our arrangement also means we made a pact to keep our playboy wiles far away from her, though truth be told, I don't know that she was ever really at risk. I'm pretty sure Kate's too smart to fall for one of us because she knows us all too well, though her gaze does seem to linger on Kennedy at times.

I grin at her. "Better. Thanks. Headache's already receding."

"Good. Because The Sams want to see you."

My grin disappears. "Now?" I check my Rolex. "It's barely eight on Monday morning."

"Yeah, well, this is Wall Street. Everyone's day started four hours ago. Speaking of which, I've called you, like, ten times."

I rub my forehead. "I lost my cell phone . . . somewhere. The Sams say what they wanted?"

"Nope," she says, bending to pull something out of a garment bag. "But they came by my desk themselves instead of sending Carla, which is never good. Put this on."

She hands me a skinny blue tie, and I obediently tug off the striped one I put on in the airport bathroom at baggage claim. At best, it smells like the smoke of a Vegas casino. At worst . . .

The way Kate wrinkles her nose when she takes it tells me it's in the unnamed "worse" category.

I put the fresh tie around my neck, but she holds up a finger and waves it in a circle. "Hmm, nope. You're worse off than I thought." She holds up a white dress shirt. "Wardrobe change. Where the hell'd you sleep last night, a barroom floor?"

"Didn't sleep at all," I mutter, unbuttoning my shirt.

It sort of sums up my and Kate's platonic relationship that I'm shirtless but she doesn't so much as glance at the upper body I've earned through long gym hours as she hands me the shirt. "One day you really are going to be too old for this, you know."

"One day," I say as I put on the fresh shirt. "Not today."

A minute later, I've got a clean shirt, new tie, and feel slightly better as the aspirin and caffeine kick in.

"The guys in?" I ask, referring to Ian and Kennedy, as I straighten the knot of my tie. I don't have a mirror, so I spread my arms for Kate to assess.

She looks me up and down. "Good as we're gonna get for now, but as soon as you're done with the meeting, you need a shower. And no, the guys aren't in. Kennedy was grabbing an early coffee with a client, and Ian said he had an early meeting as well."

I lift my eyebrows. "'Early meeting' meaning . . . he got distracted by Lara in the shower?"

"My thoughts exactly."

Ian is rather disgustingly in love with his fiancée, Lara McKenzie. And while their level of infatuation is nauseating, there's no woman I'd rather have lost my partner in playboy debauchery to than her. An agent with the white-collar division of the FBI, Lara's smart, funny, and, best of all, tolerates exactly none of Ian's bullshit, which is plentiful.

"Okay, let's do this," I say, taking one last bite of sandwich and a gulp of coffee. "Scale of one to ten, how intense were The Sams when they came by?"

"Eight," she says as we walk toward the elevators. "Here." Kate hands me a piece of gum as she punches the "Up" button.

"Where's Joe?" I ask, unwrapping the gum.

"Thailand."

"Shit," I grumble, folding the stick of gum into my mouth.

Joe Schneider is my direct boss, and he's a good one. The sort of boss you want to be by your side when the higher-ups personally summon you for something you know nothing about. No such luck today. I'd forgotten he'd taken his wife to Thailand for two weeks for their twentieth wedding anniversary.

I'm on my own.

I dutifully chew my gum until the elevator arrives, then spit it back into the wrapper so I'm not chomping gum like a sixteen-year-old cashier at the mall when I meet with the CEOs of the company.

Kate holds out her hand, but I shake my head and step into the elevator. "I don't pay you enough to throw out my chewed gum."

"You don't pay me enough for any of this," she calls after me as the elevator doors close, separating us.

It's a short ride to the top floor of the building. Can't say I spend much time up here, thank God. It's not that I mind the bosses—or my boss's bosses in this case—I just prefer my face time with them to involve one too many vodka martinis at the company holiday party.

Getting called up on a Monday morning when I'm hungover as hell? Not my idea of a solid start to the week.

Carla, the CEOs' longtime assistant, gives me a smile that's friendly but a little sympathetic. That's not good. Either I look worse than I feel or she knows something I don't.

"Hey, Carla. Are they waiting for me?"

"*Ohhh* yes," she says with a low, nervous laugh. "They're waiting for you."

"Any hints?" I ask.

She blinks. "You read the paper today?"

"Uh, no. Not yet. Which one? The *Times*? *Journal*?"

She sighs. "Oh honey . . ."

My heart beats a little faster because Carla's generally as unflappable as they come, and she looks . . . nervous.

I'm about to press her for more information when I hear my name. I glance up to see Sam Wolfe Jr. standing in the doorway of the conference room.

"Come on in, Matt." *Shit.* If Carla looks worried, Sam looks about thirty seconds away from an apoplexy.

"Sure thing," I say, forcing an easy grin as I amble into the small conference room where the other Sam is sitting at the end of the table.

Samuel and Samantha Wolfe, known as The Sams, are Wall Street's ultimate power couple. Sam inherited Wolfe Investments from his father around the same time that he married Samantha, a Wall Street powerhouse in her own right.

Neither smiles as I come in and greet them.

"Have a seat," Samantha says, gesturing at one of the available chairs.

I do as instructed, noting the newspaper on the table in front of her as I sit. I can see that it's the *Wall Street Journal* but not much else. I certainly can't figure out what the Financial District's favorite newspaper has to do with me personally.

Samantha takes charge, getting right down to business. "I assume you've read this." She sets a manicured hand on the paper.

"Ah, no. Not yet."

Sam's eyebrows go up, landing somewhere between disapproving and surprised. The *WSJ*'s required reading around here. I read it every morning, but, well, as established, today's not exactly my best morning. I haven't gotten to it yet.

Samantha lets out a long sigh as she opens the paper, turns to the second page, and refolds it before sliding it across the table.

Still baffled, I reach out and pull the paper toward me, my eyes going straight to the photo. My stomach drops as I recognize the man in the picture.

Me.

And not *just* me. Me and a scantily clad woman draped across my lap, my hands on her bare waist.

Ah hell. The memories are hazy, to say the least. The picture is from Saturday night. Or was it Friday? The photo's in black and white, but I remember the woman was blonde, the bra was red. Or was it pink? It was late by the time we got to that particular strip club; I remember that much for sure.

I drag my eyes away from the photo to the headline: HAVE THE WOLFES OF WALL STREET GONE TOO FAR?

My stomach churns. I'm used to the Wolfes of Wall Street moniker—it's all any of us at Wolfe Investments heard after the Leonardo DiCaprio movie came out. But seeing it in print alongside my face in the *Wall Street Journal* of all places . . . this isn't good.

"You must have heard about it," Sam says, his voice a low, disapproving rumble.

"No." I resist the urge to run a hand over my neck to see if I'm sweating. "I was on a red-eye." *And lost my phone somewhere in the weekend's debauchery.*

Sam grunts, then exchanges a long look with his wife. In my hungover state, I'm not at the top of my game, but I still know that look doesn't mean good things.

Samantha's the one to give it to me straight. "You can read the full article later, but I'll give you the highlights: You stumbled into the same club as a *WSJ* reporter who was covering a story in Vegas. He was sober. You were not. You were seen tucking hundreds into G-strings, dropping thousands on a single round of expensive whiskey, and that wasn't even your last stop of the evening. He followed you to three other clubs, where members of your party unabashedly partook in illegal substances."

My head snaps up. "I don't touch drugs. Booze, sure, but that's it."

"Booze and women," Sam says with a pointed look at the paper.

"Lap dances aren't illegal. Neither's vodka or whiskey."

Still, I get their point. I'm hardly a saint, but the weekend in Vegas had gotten crazy, even by my standards. My cousin's a big-shot club owner in Miami, and his group of friends had not only taken partying to a whole other level but also been cocky about it. Cocky and stupid, and now, apparently, I'm to pay the price for that stupidity just by association.

"No, you weren't technically caught doing anything illegal," Samantha grants. "And we're not here to act as your parents. You're one of our best, Matt, you know that. But this is bad. We've already received a half dozen calls from concerned clients, wondering just what the hell we're doing with their money."

"I spend *my* money," I say, stabbing a finger against the newsprint. "And I've earned every penny."

"We know that," Samantha says. "But you know as well as we do that perception often counts more than fact. Nobody's going to believe you didn't touch the cocaine. Nobody's going to believe the hundreds you threw at these women stopped at a harmless lap dance. Drugs, prostitution, reckless spending . . . those aren't accusations we can weather easily. Especially not after the insider-trading allegations against Ian last year. We're still doing damage control from that."

"He was found innocent," I snap, ever defensive of my friend who may be a bit of a daredevil, but who plays strictly by the book when it comes to his work.

"Yes. Officially," Sam says. "But as we said, there's the perception issue. And this . . ." He gestures at the paper and breaks off.

Samantha folds her hands on the table and meets my eyes. "Public relations and legal have strongly suggested that we let you go to ward off the worst of the reputation hit."

For a second, I think I've heard her wrong. "Excuse me?"

"We don't see the need to take it that far," Samantha says, pausing to let an unspoken *yet* linger in the silence. "We understand this was a bit of bad luck on your part, being in the same club as a reporter. But Matt, we do have to do some damage control here. You've already had two clients request to be moved to another broker."

Shit. Seriously? I'm torn between incredulity and anger—first, at the fact that it's happening at all, and second, that it's turning into a big fucking deal. I manage to nod, even as my racing brain is in denial. "What kind of damage control?"

Samantha looks at her husband, who takes over. "We're thinking an image overhaul."

"A what?"

"You know . . ." He waves his hand. "Cutting back on the booze. Limiting the late nights. Skipping the caviar at dinner. Keeping your bar bill under four figures. And for the love of God, avoiding the strip club and your cocaine-loving friends."

"Sure, of course," I hear myself say, even when I feel a bit like puking. I don't know if it's from the bucket of booze I had just a few hours earlier or the situation at hand. Likely a combination of both.

"There's another thing," Samantha says. "All of this will help, but nothing signals a reformed man like a plus-one. I mean, look at Ian and Lara. He was even more wild than you, and now he's—"

"Domesticated, I know," I snap. "But he didn't plan for that; it just happened. I don't have a Lara McKenzie waiting in the wings. I'm single and happy to be."

"Well, get un-single," Samantha says, standing as though that's the end of the conversation. "Preferably in time for the Wolfe Annual Gala next month."

"Wait, what? What do you mean?"

Sam stands and moves so he's beside his wife with a grin. "She means that nothing cleans up a man's reputation like the right woman by his side."

"But—"

Samantha pins me with a look. "I'll spell it out for you, Matt. Get a girlfriend."

"Or?" I ask, sensing an ultimatum at play.

She gives a thin smile. "Or get a new job."

2

Sabrina

Monday Morning, September 18

Weather-wise, it's the perfect morning.

Just warm enough to enjoy a cappuccino on my favorite restaurant's patio, just crisp enough to warrant the new cashmere sweater I bought to usher in the fall weather.

A little *less* perfect? The expression on Lorna Midler's face right now as she flips through a dozen photos of her in twelve different sexual positions with her personal trainer.

She looks devastated, and even though I've been at this career for years and am a die-hard cynic, it's difficult not to feel somewhat sorry for her.

To give her a bit of privacy, I lift my mug and study the little heart the barista made in the foam, smiling because the gesture, while sweet, proves he or she doesn't know me at all.

True love? Not really my thing.

See? Cynic.

Lorna pushes her Chanel glasses atop her head to stare at me, aghast. "You can't be serious, Sabrina. How did you get these?"

Her voice is sharp and aggressive. She's moved from devastated to defensive, fast.

I keep my own voice soothing to counter her anger. "I didn't climb a tree outside your Park Avenue brownstone, if that's what you're asking."

"But you hired someone else to? What, you paid some sleazy PI so you could ruin my marriage?"

I take a sip of the cappuccino, the foam heart dissolving into a blur as I resist the urge to point out that *she* ruined her marriage.

"I understand this is frustrating," I say, keeping my voice calm.

Lorna snorts. "How can you possibly understand? Have you ever been married?"

It's my turn to snort, though I do so in my head, not out loud. Marriage has never been part of my life's plan, and relationships like Lorna's are part of the reason why.

"I can sue you," Lorna hisses at me when I don't reply.

I don't even flinch. It's a common threat, and one that holds no weight. "For your sake, I wouldn't recommend it. We signed a contract that clearly states—"

"That you work for me!"

I continue over her outburst. "That in order to retain my services, you must be completely forthcoming." I pull a copy of said contract out of my bag, sliding it in front of her. "If you flip to page two, you'll note section 3A and your initials, where you agreed to answer my questions honestly. Section 3B, also initialed, is where you agreed to forfeit your deposit if at any time you lie to me during the course of our business."

"I never—"

I hold up one hand to stop her, then pull out a small recorder from my bag and set it on the table. "This is our session from Bemelmans. The one where you told me point-blank that you'd been faithful to your husband."

She glares, but I refuse to back down.

"Lorna, I didn't take the photos. You hired me to investigate your husband, and that's precisely what I set out to do. But your husband either knew about or anticipated your plan, because the second I entered his office, he handed me the envelope with those very photos. Taken two days *before* you lied to me about your fidelity."

She fiddles with her necklace. "You spoke with him?"

"I did. I prefer to deal with people directly. To look them in the eye, gauge their physical response to my questions. In this case, he was one step ahead of me. He not only knew that you had an affair, he had proof."

She swallows nervously. "So what happens now?"

"I strongly suggest you and your husband sit down and have a conversation. If not with each other, at least with your respective attorneys. This is beyond me now."

"But I hired you to ensure I didn't lose everything in the divorce!"

"No, you hired me to determine the nature of your husband's philandering. You neglected to mention your own, which is a breach of our contract."

"Fine," she snaps, folding the contract back up and tossing it across the table at me in disgust. She reaches behind to pull her Gucci purse off the back of her chair and sets it in her lap. "I wish I could say good riddance, but I'll likely see you again, won't I?"

I reach out and pick up the recorder, putting it back in my bag. "I do tend to run into my past clients socially, yes."

She laughs. "You know, I've never really thought about it until now, but you must be the most powerful woman in Manhattan. Just how many New York secrets do you have access to?"

I shrug and give her an honest response. "Plenty."

Her answering smile is tight and unfriendly. "Yes. Well. Just as long as they stay secrets."

I pat the papers still on the table. "I signed the contract, too. And I always uphold my end."

She stands and gathers up the stack of photos. "I'll be keeping these."

I wave a hand. *By all means.* She and I both know there are duplicates. Multiple sets, hard copies, and digital files.

Lorna walks away without a word, all skinny shoulders and hip wiggles as she saunters down Spring Street. She's left me with the bill, but with what I charge, I can surely pay for her mimosa.

I know. You're thinking I'm someone who thrives on other people's problems.

Sort of.

But I offer them solutions. For a price, yes, but I don't deal in extortion. I'm upfront with how I work and what they can expect from me from the very beginning.

There are no "gotchas," at least from me.

See, I'm a fixer. Which is basically a fancy way of saying I handle the messy shit that people get themselves into. Your worst dirty laundry? I can manage it. Your darkest secrets? I can work with those. But only if you tell me . . . *up front.*

I don't give a crap that Lorna Midler was banging her beefcake trainer. Goodness knows her husband was no saint.

But I care that she kept it from me.

I've dealt with all sorts of morally bankrupt people in my line of work. Cheaters. Adulterers. Even people who've got a toe on the other side of the law. It's all part of the job, and it's a job I like.

But I refuse to work with liars.

I mentally add Lorna to my blacklist—not that I'll snub her when we inevitably run into each other socially. But we won't be working together in the future.

"Ms. Cross, another cappuccino?" I glance up and smile at Javier, one of the regular servers.

"I'm at my caffeine quota for the day. How about one of your herbal teas? Surprise me on the flavor. Oh, and the paper, please."

He nods, and I sit back in my chair, inhaling the fresh air with its hint of autumn as I take in the quiet SoHo foot traffic. The neighborhood boasts some of the city's best shopping, but it's too early in the day for the shops to be open, so the streets are quiet, the peacefulness interrupted only by New York's ever-present taxi horns.

"Here we are, Ms. Cross," Javier says, approaching with a pot of hot water and a floral china teacup. "No cream or sugar, correct?"

"Good memory," I say as he pours steaming water into the cup.

He sets the pot on the table, as well as my newspaper and a croissant, which he delivers with a wink. "On the house."

I don't bother to tell him that *on the house* doesn't mean the calories in the buttery confection won't end up on my hips and that free food doesn't often translate to fat-free.

Still, I nibble the corner of the pastry after he walks away, because it beats the hell out of the nonfat Greek yogurt I had earlier. I've been determined to teach myself to like the stuff, but so far, no luck. It may be healthy, but it's also sour and doesn't come close to beating a flaky croissant.

I wipe my buttery fingers on my napkin and pick up the *Wall Street Journal.* I get the *WSJ* and a half dozen other newspapers delivered to my apartment every morning, and I read them cover to cover. Staying informed is paramount to doing my job well. But my meeting with Lorna was early, and I didn't have time to finish my usual reading.

I sip my tea as I scan the front page. A moderate earthquake in the Bay Area, no reported injuries, thank goodness. Politicians at an international peace summit. A tech giant with another record-breaking quarter . . .

I turn the page.

And nearly drop my teacup.

"Oh my *God*." I lean closer to the paper, making sure it's really him, but . . . of course it is.

Even without his name in the description, who else would be in the *Wall Street Journal*, straddled by a half-naked woman with her back to the camera?

Who else would have his hand on her waist, his grin as cocky as ever?

Who else, besides Matt Cannon, would ruin my appetite for a perfectly good croissant?

Because that's what Matt Cannon does. He turns my otherwise in-control life upside down, every damn chance he gets.

3

MATT

Tuesday Morning, September 19

"So, what are you going to do?" Kennedy asks, his eyes watching the bar I'm benching as he spots me.

"Hell if I know," I manage with gritted teeth as I push through the rep. "Know any rent-a-girlfriend services?"

"None that aren't glorified escort services and won't get you into more trouble."

"I don't think that's even possible," I say, finishing the last rep in my set and letting Kennedy guide the weight back to its resting place.

I sit up, and my other best friend, Ian, tosses me a towel, which I catch with one hand.

Ian sits on the bench opposite mine, hands clasped loosely between his knees. "I sent you a fucking million texts yesterday. You didn't reply."

I wipe my face with the towel. "Sorry. The Sams figured everyone would be buzzing, and that I'd be better working from home."

"Everyone *was* buzzing," Kennedy says. "Still doesn't explain why you ignored us."

"Not intentional," I grumble. "I was on the phone all day doing damage control with clients, and then I turned off my phone last night to . . . I dunno. Think."

What I *don't* tell them is that those conversations were a hell of a lot rougher than I'd anticipated. My bosses weren't exaggerating. This is bad. *Really* bad.

The guys nod without bugging me further, and I'm grateful for the understanding. Or at least the temporary free pass on not talking about it.

We all belong to the same gym, but it's rare for us to be here at the same time. The guys did a decent job of playing innocent, but I sense they showed up at the same time because of me—*for* me.

The three of us started at Wolfe Investments at the same time, six years ago. Me as a twenty-two-year-old cocky brat with a brain for numbers, them a couple of years older, a little less whiz kid but no less cocky.

With as cutthroat as Wall Street is, it's a wonder the three of us didn't end up killing each other on our way to the top. Instead, we rose to the top together, competing, sure, but in a way that pushed each other to be better. No, the best. Because damn it, we *are* the best.

Guess the cockiness didn't fade with age.

Kennedy leans on the bar, a water bottle dangling from his hands, looking unflappable as he always does. He's the serious, old-fashioned one of our group, the type of guy who you should never challenge to a game of Scrabble or chess, and whose first word was probably *mahogany*, or some shit.

Ian's charming, confident, and the most determined, stubborn son-of-a-bitch I know. He had a shitty time of it growing up, but he took all the crap of his childhood and used it as fuel to put himself through Yale and elbow his way in with the Wall Street hotshots.

Me? Well, I've already mentioned the whole boy-wonder crap. My brain's sort of a human calculator of sorts, but my parents did a decent job of not letting me nerd out. I was equally good at math and football, and, well, how do I put this . . .

My life's always been damn good. Easy.

Until . . .

Now, apparently.

"So it's that bad?" Ian asks.

I drag the towel over my damp face once more. "Worse. Since I met with The Sams yesterday morning, a half dozen other clients have called to 'express their concerns.'" I put air quotes around the last part.

"Oh, come on. Who hasn't done something crazy at a bachelor party?" Ian scoffs. Kennedy nods in commiseration.

I rest my elbows on my knees and let my chin drop toward my chest for a second. Much as I appreciate my friends' loyalty, at the moment, it does nothing to solve my problem.

I know that what I do in my free time doesn't affect my work. I know that I'm one of the best damn brokers at Wolfe. *I* know that my clients' money is safe, that I can do my job in my sleep and do it well. But it turns out The Sams were right. Perception is everything, and right now, I've got a serious image problem.

"What about Lara?" Kennedy asks Ian. "She got any friends who want to play the part of Mrs. Cannon?"

Oh hell no.

I hold up a hand. "Easy there. The bosses said I need a girlfriend, not a *wife*."

"Yeah, but for this to work, people have to believe there's a *chance* this woman could be your wife. It's about you settling down."

"I don't need to settle down," I say, agitatedly running my hands through my hair. "I need everyone else to get their heads out of their asses and quit blowing this out of proportion."

"Look," Ian says with a sigh. "If anyone knows what it's like to have his life turned upside down overnight, it's me. I understand even more what it's like to have accusations hurled at you that are unfounded. You want to fight, and I get that. But you've also got to ask yourself what you want more: to stand on principle or your job."

I look back up. "You're saying I should give in? Play along?"

"I'm saying, there are worse things than pretending to have a girlfriend for a few weeks until this blows over. Nobody's asking you to walk down the aisle or go diamond shopping. Just let people think that you might consider doing it . . . someday."

I grunt, not in the mood to get into all the reasons why I have zero intention of walking down the aisle or going diamond shopping—*ever.*

"Ian's right. Things could be worse. Like having the SEC on your ass for insider trading," Kennedy says with a bland look at Ian.

Ian glares. "*Alleged* insider trading. And I was cleared."

Kennedy's hands lift in surrender. "I know. I was just trying to back up your point that Matt's situation could be worse."

They're right. I feel like an ass complaining about my situation when it's nothing compared to what Ian went through.

His worst-case scenario had been prison; mine's . . . what? Playing house for a few weeks? Pretending to be a doting boyfriend? It's a small price to pay for keeping the life I've worked for—the life I love.

"Okay, fine," I say, draping the towel around my neck as I look at Ian. "Kennedy's right. Lara's my best bet for finding a woman to play the part."

Ian's blue eyes blink. "How the hell do you figure that?"

"Because she's the only nice girl we know."

"Kate's nice," Ian points out.

"I don't think the guy who bones his assistant is what the bosses had in mind when they suggested this plan," Kennedy points out. "Lara's social group's a better bet."

"Am I the only one who remembers that my fiancée is FBI?" Ian asks incredulously. "Lying isn't really their thing."

"Sure it is. They do undercover work," I argue.

"They go undercover to solve crimes and catch bad guys," Ian says. "Not save party-boy reputations. No offense."

"None taken," I say, knowing he's right. "What about that Gabby chick, Lara's best friend?"

"Moved to Paris with her boyfriend. A long-distance fake girlfriend's not going to do you any good. What about her friend Megan, the cute redhead from her yoga class? You met her at our dinner party last month."

I immediately shake my head. Not that Megan wasn't cute and fun and all that, but she gave off a distinct vibe that she was looking for more than a fling. The type of girl who wants to find a boyfriend who turns into a husband who turns into a dad. None of that's for me, which is why I'd politely avoided her all evening.

"Too risky," I say.

Kennedy raises his eyebrows. "Risky? That woman was five two if an inch and as likable as they come."

"Exactly," I say, standing and gripping the towel around my neck with both hands and tugging in aggravation over this whole situation. "That's exactly my problem. You guys know as well as I do what it's like to be a single millionaire under thirty . . . five," I add with a glance at a glowering Kennedy, remembering he's got a few years on me. "At the risk of sounding like a conceited asshole . . ."

"You don't know any women who can pretend to be your girlfriend without actually wanting the part?" Ian asks.

"Not really, no. And while I can think of a handful who'd be game to play along, I wouldn't trust any of them to know how to conduct themselves in a business meeting. They'd probably order shots at dinner and end up doing more harm than good."

"So no marriage-minded women, but no party girls, either," Kennedy muses.

"Right. I need someone who will know the stakes from the very beginning and who won't misconstrue anything when I act besotted with her in front of clients."

"Did you just use the word *besotted*?" Ian asks.

I hitch my thumb at Kennedy. "His dopey vocabulary is rubbing off on me. But you guys get what I mean, right?"

"Yeah, you're not wrong," Kennedy says as the three of us make our way over to the squat rack that's finally freed up. "It doesn't help that the light at the end of the tunnel is the Wolfe Gala. You're going to have to convince a hell of a lot of people you're in love, all while champagne and absurdly expensive dresses are involved."

"What do dresses have to do with anything?" I ask.

"The Cinderella complex," Ian chimes in as he adds weight to the rack.

I stare at him, then Kennedy. "The what now?"

"You know." Kennedy waves his hand impatiently. "The whole princess-ball thing. Fancy dresses, chandeliers. Dancing."

"What the hell do you two watch in your downtime? How about more sports, less Disney Channel?"

Ian shrugs and steps into the rack. "Fine. Go ahead and risk it."

I grimace, because the scene they just described is exactly what I'm trying to avoid.

"Unless . . . ," Kennedy says.

I glance at him. "I'll take an unless. What've you got?"

"You're not going to like it."

"I'll like anything better than your Snow White scenario."

"Cinderella," Ian corrects.

"Whatever. Kennedy, talk to me."

Instead of answering, Kennedy looks at Ian, and I know these two guys well enough to know that whatever they're about to launch at me, it's been their plan all along.

"Shit. What?" I say impatiently.

"You need someone to play along who has zero risk of emotional entanglements," Ian says slowly.

I roll my finger to speed him along. "Yes, we've covered that. You know someone?"

"We all know her," Ian says, holding my gaze.

The answer hits me like a kick to the balls.

Sabrina Cross.

Ian's friend since childhood, Sabrina's an annoying constant in our social circle.

My friends are right. She is the last woman on earth to be at risk of falling for me. Because Sabrina Cross hates my guts.

4

Sabrina

Tuesday Night, September 19

Quiet nights at home are rare in my line of work. More often than not, I'm in four-inch heels and a little black dress at fancy fund-raisers, cocktail parties, or expensive dinners.

In other words, nights out on the town? Part of the job. People think they're paying me big money to solve their problems, and technically they are, but what they're *really* paying for are my connections and how well I know people.

Name a judge: I know her favorite type of French wine. Name an attorney: I know his phone number and his niece's birthday. Name a socialite: I can give you a list of every person she's ever dated. Name a hedge fund manager: I can tell you the name of his wife and his mistress.

I don't have a little black book; I've got an entire encyclopedia, and there's nothing little about it.

The point is, a night to myself is rare, and when they come up, I go all in. Yoga pants, fuzzy socks, oversize sweatshirt, messy bun, Norah Jones on the speakers, the works.

Normally I pour myself a big old glass of red wine and settle in for a movie, and though a movie's still on the agenda, I'm not feeling the red wine vibe tonight. It feels like a cocktail kind of evening.

I feed my dog, Juno, and begin setting out the makings for an ice-cold martini, when someone knocks on my front door, setting Juno into a barking frenzy.

I scrunch my nose at the interruption. Not only because I'm not expecting anyone, and I *hate* the unexpected, but because I live in a high-rise on the Upper East Side where the doormen look like bouncers. Nobody gets up here without being on a resident's preapproved list. I can count the number of people on my list on one hand, and none of them is expected tonight.

Going to the door, I check the peephole, assuming it'll be someone who knocked on the wrong door by accident.

I groan, because it's so much worse than an accident.

I purse my lips and consider my options. I could pretend I'm not here, but remember before when I said that I know people?

Well, I know this guy better than most. He's relentless. And he *will* wait me out.

Giving in to the inevitable, I open my front door, not bothering to hold Juno back from throwing her considerable weight at Matt Cannon.

Instead of looking annoyed by the eighty pounds of Lab / Rottweiler mix getting fur all over his thousand-dollar suit, Matt bends down and gives Juno an affectionate rubdown. "Hey, girl."

I lean against the doorjamb, begrudging my dog her poor taste in character. "How'd you get in here?"

Juno rolls onto her back, tongue lolling out, belly up, and Matt obliges, scratching the dog like they're old friends. "Doorman let me up."

"You're not on the list."

"You sure about that?" he says with a grin. Then he looks up at me and does a double take at my appearance. "Whoa. Has it finally happened? Have you finally run out of skin-tight dresses and high heels?"

"What did you think, I slept in a push-up bra and Louboutins?"

His grin shifts from playful to seductive. "I know firsthand that you don't."

I bite the inside of my cheek to keep from saying that in the few times he's seen me in my bra—and out of it—we don't exactly do much sleeping.

Because of that, I'm relieved at my current appearance. The casual clothes feel like a shield of sorts—a guarantee that he won't make his move and that I won't be helpless to resist, as I generally am.

Matt gives my dog one last pet and stands. His six-foot-two frame doesn't quite tower over my five-foot-seven self, but I have to look up, and that's annoying.

Actually, everything about him is annoying.

See, adversaries aren't supposed to look like him. And make no mistake, for all our ill-advised hookups in the past, Matt *is* an adversary. As such, it'd only be fair for him to have scars, a paunch, or at least an asymmetrical face.

He's got none of the above. Simply and reluctantly put, men don't come better-looking than Matt Cannon. He's the epitome of a golden boy. Perfectly styled blond hair? Check. Mischievous blue eyes? Yup. Chiseled jaw? Uh-huh. Perfect body . . .

Yeah, you get the idea.

Also, I hate him.

I lean against my doorjamb, still blocking his entry. "Why are you here, and why in God's name did my doorman let you up?"

Matt puts a hand to my waist as though it's his right and nudges me aside so he can enter my apartment. As though that's his right, too. Juno follows him in happily.

"You were in Baltimore last month," he says.

I blink in confusion at the change of subject. "And?"

"You asked Kate to watch Juno, except she went out to Jersey to have brunch with her parents, and the train broke down. Your dog needed to go out, so . . . I came over. Juno and I hit it off, so I took over dog-sitting duties for the weekend."

I stare at him, aghast. "Just like that. You were in my apartment. Watching my dog."

He looks down at me. "Don't be weird about it. I've been in your apartment before."

"Yeah, for dinner parties. Under supervision. And when . . ."

His eyebrows lift. "Yes?"

I refuse to blush, and I refuse to answer. I don't particularly care to think about the times my body's desire for this man has overridden common sense, resulting in a hookup or two. Or twelve. And I *definitely* don't talk about it.

His cocky wink tells me he knows exactly what I'm thinking, but for once, he doesn't give me shit. Instead, he turns to survey my apartment.

"I've never mentioned this before, but I like your place. Juno and I made ourselves at home while I watched her."

"Juno *was* home," I point out. "You were an uninvited intruder."

He ignores this. "Your home suits you."

"I'm assuming there's an insult in there somewhere?" I ask over my shoulder, heading back into the kitchen.

"Nope, I really do like it. It's the only thing I like about you," he says, following me.

I ignore the barb, since it's sort of what we do. Plus . . . I like my place, too. It's on the forty-second floor, right on Park Avenue, and the view alone is worth the astronomical rent.

I'm also pretty proud to say I've made a home out of what could have been a generic mausoleum. The leather sofa's gray and warm and comfortable, with inviting red throw pillows. Instead of a coffee table,

I've got an enormous ottoman, with a tray for cocktails and scented candles.

There's a wine rack in one corner of the living room, a dog bed in the other, and the rest is all windows with a glorious view of the Empire State Building, the bright lights of downtown twinkling off in the distance.

The kitchen, too, is inviting, at least by Manhattan standards, since we New Yorkers aren't exactly known for our cooking skills.

Juno dashes for her beloved, albeit slightly decrepit, squeaky sheep-shaped toy and takes to her dog bed, and I watch out of the corner of my eye as Matt comes to join me in the kitchen.

He's wearing a suit, which isn't all that surprising—he's pretty much always wearing a suit. This one's a dark gray, and the blue tie matches his eyes, though a medieval torture chamber wouldn't get me to admit that I notice.

Out of habit, or instinct, or maybe just poor judgment, I measure the ingredients for two martinis, one for each of us. I've just added the vodka and vermouth to the shaker when Matt comes around the counter.

Wordlessly, he plucks the shaker out of my hands and takes over.

It's a high-handed move, and completely like him. But whereas I'd normally protest on principle, I let him do it, sensing that he needs the control more than I do tonight.

Something's on his mind—he wouldn't be here otherwise—and based on what I saw in the *WSJ* yesterday, I've got a pretty good sense of what that something is.

Matt goes to my freezer and adds ice, as though it's the most natural thing in the world for him to be in my kitchen, making the two of us cocktails.

He puts the lid on the shaker, but before shaking it, he sets it aside and shrugs out of his suit jacket, tossing it onto the back of one of the dining room chairs, then rolls up his sleeves.

My mouth goes a little dry at the sight of white sleeves being rolled over tanned male forearms, but I refuse to respond or even look interested.

Thankfully the sound of the cocktail shaker defuses the sexual tension. Or so I tell myself as I pull two cocktail glasses off my bar cart and set them in front of him.

Matt strains the drink into both glasses. He adds three olives to mine, exactly as I like it, then grabs a lemon from the fruit bowl on my counter, adding a citrus twist to his, exactly as *he* likes it.

He hands me mine, lifts his in a toast. "Cheers."

"To . . . your newfound notoriety?" I say, clinking my glass to his before taking a sip.

"You saw the paper."

"Cannon, everyone saw that paper," I say, taking my cocktail into the living room and dropping onto a soft leather chair.

He follows, sitting on the edge of the couch, and reaches for a coaster before putting down his drink. I have no doubt it's a spillover from his upper-middle-class upbringing. He's not quite as upper crust as his friend Kennedy Dawson, whose blood is as blue as it gets. But from what I've been able to piece together, Matt's childhood in the Connecticut suburbs was a far cry from my early life in Philly.

Juno dashes over and jumps up on the couch beside him, something she usually does only with me.

Matt rubs Juno's head, looking at the dog instead of at me, and I decide it's time to cut the bull. "When do we get to the point about what you're doing here?"

He smiles without looking at me. "Usually a woman asks that before making her visitor a drink."

"I took pity on you. The *WSJ*, remember?"

His smile disappears. "Hard to forget."

"So." I sip my drink. "Vegas."

He runs his hands over his face and slumps back against the couch. “It was Troy’s bachelor party.”

“Troy?”

“My cousin. Kind of a douchebag now, but we had some fun memories growing up.”

“So if it was *his* bachelor party, why wasn’t he the one with a naked woman draped over his lap?”

“He was,” Matt grumbles. “He just wasn’t featured in the *Wall Street Journal*.”

Much as Matt drives me crazy, it’s hard not to feel a little sorry for the guy. I can’t even fathom the horror of *anyone* seeing me at a vulnerable moment, let alone millions of *WSJ* subscribers.

“I didn’t sleep with her.”

I blink, thrown off by the unexpected pronouncement. “I didn’t ask. And in no way is that my business.”

He shrugs and leans forward, picking up his drink.

I take a deep breath. I meant what I said. What Matt does in his spare time, with other women . . . totally not my business.

We’re not dating. We don’t even like each other. We’re simply two people who, against their better judgment, sleep together, with each ill-fated naked encounter somehow driving us further apart instead of closer together.

But still, we’re not exclusive.

And yet . . . there’s relief that he didn’t sleep with the Vegas stripper, or whatever she was.

I hate myself for it, but it’s there. Relief, pure and strong and absolutely not to be analyzed.

“The bosses are pissed?” I ask.

Matt grunts his assent, taking another sip of his martini.

“It’ll pass,” I say. “Some other scandal will come up, and the whole thing will blow over.”

He stands and goes to the window, taking his cocktail with him as he studies the Manhattan skyline. "They've given me an ultimatum."

"Seriously?" I ask. "It's that bad?" I'm surprised. Even I know what an asset he is to Wolfe Investments, with that big number-crunching brain of his.

Matt shoves his free hand in his pocket and doesn't turn around. "Just a perfect-storm situation, I think. The fact that the story broke in a prestigious newspaper instead of *Page Six*. The fact that some of the morons I was with were into the hard stuff but the reporter failed to mention that I didn't touch the cocaine. Plus, Wolfe's still recovering from Ian's scandal. The higher-ups are on edge."

"So they're going to fire you for getting a lap dance?" I ask incredulously. "Unless you do what?"

"They want me to settle down."

I snort. "Have they actually met you?"

"Ian settled down. He was even more wild than me."

I stare at his back. "You're serious. You're going to do this?"

"No, *they're* serious," he says, turning back to me with no trace of his usual cocky smile. "I get a girlfriend, or I get canned."

I ignore the little stab of something painful in my chest at the thought of Matt committed to someone for the long haul, the way Ian and Lara are.

I take a sip of my cocktail as I think this over.

His situation sucks, and his life needs fixing. That's what I do. I'm actually not all that surprised he showed up, though I sort of imagined his request for help would be along the lines of getting the *WSJ* to issue a retraction.

At this rate, though, even if I could achieve that, I don't know what good it would do. This city, this life, is all about reputation. Once it's smeared, you can't undo the smear. You simply have to smear it with something else. Something better.

Like a girlfriend.

Much as I hate to admit it, the plan has merit. Nothing takes the steam out of a playboy scandal like a ball and chain.

"You want my help."

He takes a sip of his drink and stays silent.

I push him. "C'mon, Cannon, admit it. You never come here. We never do drinks just the two of us, unless it's after . . . you know."

His eyebrows go up. "Sex?"

"Right. Which is absolutely not on the agenda."

The corner of his mouth turns up. "Figured that from your attire."

I glance down. "What's wrong with my outfit?"

"Nothing. I just didn't know you owned a sweatshirt, much less purple socks."

"Do you live in your suit?"

"No." Another sip of his cocktail. "Sometimes I'm naked."

The picture of exactly what his perfect body looks like flits through my mind, and I push it aside. "You're changing the subject," I say, setting my glass on the table. No coaster. "What do you want?"

"Shit, Sabrina, you already know what I want. I want to hire you."

"You need a girlfriend. A fake one," I say, making sure I understand the request.

"Yup. For the next month or so, I need to be completely enamored with a woman. And I need her to pretend to be devoted to me."

"Vegas warts and all," I murmur as I contemplate his bosses' ultimatum.

"You think the plan is crap?" he asks.

I feel a jolt of pleasure—of pride—when I realize he's really asking. That he really wants my opinion on something this important to him.

"Actually . . . no," I say slowly, chewing an olive. "I've discovered that a man can get away with just about anything so long as the same woman appears on his arm at the right society events."

He sighs. "I was kind of hoping you'd tell me the plan was total shit so I wouldn't have to go through with it."

"Not excited about having a little lady in your life?" I keep my voice light and joking, carefully hiding the relief that he's in no hurry to settle down, even just for pretend. It helps ease the sting of what he's about to ask me to do:

Find him his fake girlfriend.

Even knowing it won't be real, the thought of finding some perfect woman to be his ally for the next month . . .

I shove the regret aside. "Okay, so, your fake girlfriend. How long do I have to find her?"

"Ah . . ."

I frown at his discomfort. "You just said you need to hire me. You need me to fix this, right?"

"Yeah, but . . ." He drags a hand down his face.

"What am I missing?" I ask, my heart pounding just a little in anticipation of something coming my way that I'm not going to like. "You need a girlfriend; I'll find you a girlfriend."

"I don't want a girlfriend. I mean, I do, but . . ." He lifts his head and locks his gaze with mine. "I want you."

"What?"

"I want you to play the part, Sabrina. No, that's not right." He looks down quickly, then meets my eyes again. "I *need* you."

My breath goes out on a whoosh.

I've heard him wrong. *Surely* I've heard him wrong.

The air seems to go still, as though we're in some weird alternate-universe vortex. Because an alternate universe is the only scenario in which he'd ask me that. Or that I'd consider saying yes.

"No," I say. "No freaking way."

He sighs, as though I'm being unreasonable. "I'm not asking you to go steady, Sabrina, just . . . pretend."

"Doesn't matter. Not interested." I snatch up both our glasses and head to the kitchen. *Conversation over.*

"Double your rate. I can afford it."

"I don't doubt it, but this isn't about money."

"Then what is it about?" he asks, following me into the kitchen.

"We'd destroy each other," I say, whirling around to face him. "Surely you realize that."

He runs a hand down his face again. "I do realize that, but I'm short on options."

I snort. "Please. I could come up with a dozen women who'd die for the part. Most of them we wouldn't even have to pay."

He and I both stiffen a bit at my words, recalling a night years ago, the night that started us on our path to destruction.

Matt touches my arm. "Sabrina."

"I don't accept money in exchange for my company," I say quietly, shrugging off his touch. "You of all people know that."

"I do know that, but I'm also desperate," he says, his voice urgent. "I need someone who knows the score. Someone who I won't have to worry about getting the wrong idea. Someone who I can part ways with after my image is restored, no worse for wear."

"And you think that's me? Your mortal enemy?"

"I want you *because* you're my mortal enemy, Sabrina."

"Why?"

His eyes lock on mine. "Because of all the women in my life, you're the one I can count on to never fall in love with me."

5

Matt

Tuesday Night, September 19

When I first met Sabrina Cross, I thought she was the most beautiful woman I'd ever seen.

Four years later?

I still think it.

The woman's a perfect ten. Fantasy-worthy curves. Her long coffee-brown hair is streaked with gold, her eyes piercing and blue, her features as feminine as they are stubborn.

She's also a royal pain in the ass.

I hate that I find her attractive, but I thought I'd resigned myself to the fact.

Tonight, however, my attraction to her is trickier.

For starters, she's not even remotely trying to be hot. Her hair's in a messy knot, makeup washed off for the night. Her pants, while sinfully tight, are of the comfortable "night at home" variety. And I wasn't lying about my surprise at the sweatshirt.

I've only ever seen Sabrina in tight dresses or slinky negligees.

This version's . . . softer. And absurdly appealing.

But you know what's not soft? My cock.

Also, the murderous glint in her eyes.

"No way. No way in hell." She puts her glass on the counter and reaches for the vodka, clearly intending to make herself another drink.

I pull the bottle of Grey Goose from her hand and begin to make us each another martini.

We're going to fucking need it.

"I just need you for a month," I say, trying to keep the impatience out of my voice. "People will believe it. We've known each other for years, and it'd be more plausible that Ian set us up than me suddenly dating some new thing. Plus, I can count on you not to get . . . the Cinderella complex or whatever."

Sabrina blinks. "Cinderella what?"

"You know . . . fancy dresses, the ball . . ."

Her eyes go wide. "Ball?"

"Gala. The Wolfe Gala. I need you to go with me."

She laughs and hands me the vermouth bottle. "Of course you do."

Okay. So she's going to be a hard sell. I was prepared for that.

I measure the vermouth, dump it into the shaker, and turn toward her. "Triple your rate."

She shakes her head emphatically. "I don't need money."

No. She doesn't. Her place is nearly as lavish as my own, and even if it wasn't, she's not the type of woman who does anything for financial gain. I learned that in a big way four years ago, and I paid the ultimate price:

Her.

"Okay, forget the money," I say, going to the ice maker and filling the shaker. "What do you want?"

She tilts her head. "What do you mean?"

"There's got to be something you want. If money doesn't incentivize you, name something that does."

"Your head on a silver platter?"

I ignore this and keep my attention on the cocktails. "Seriously. Name your price."

She fishes an olive out of the jar and pops it into her mouth. "Seriously. You have nothing I want."

I could kiss her sassy mouth, lick the salty olive brine off her lips, and prove her a liar. But right now, there's something I need more than her body, though barely.

I set the lid on the shaker and pound it shut with a punch of my fist, harder than necessary. The woman's damn stubborn.

I lift it to my shoulder and shake it with all the frustration coursing through my body. Frustration over the idiots in Vegas, the dipshit from the *WSJ*, the fact that my bosses and my clients can't see past the drama of it all.

That I have to rely on someone other than myself to save my job.

That it's *this* woman in particular who can save my job.

But then, that's not exactly true. Sabrina's right. I could find someone else. I could probably even find someone who would keep her emotional distance.

The truth is, I don't want someone else. I want someone I can trust, and though I'd rather die than admit it to her, I trust Sabrina.

We say nothing as she spears three olives and drops the cocktail pick into her glass. We both reach for the lemon at the same time, my hand closing over hers.

Another woman might have jerked her hand back, but there's nothing twitchy or hesitant about Sabrina Cross. Instead she looks at me, lifting her eyebrows. *Back off.*

I remove my hand from hers slowly, letting my fingertips linger on the back of her smooth skin before withdrawing.

She takes her time with the lemon twist, peeling the citrus carefully and setting it on my glass with precision.

"I don't want anything from you," she says again, and my stomach twists in resignation. "But . . . I can find you someone perfect for the job. Someone more perfect than me. You have to trust me on this. This is what I *do*, Matt. Not only do I fix things, I know how to fix them. And I know plenty of single women who are perfect marriage material. They'll—"

"No," I interrupt. "I don't want marriage material."

On this, I'm very, very clear. As someone with no intentions of ever getting married, I refuse to lead on any woman who *does* want that.

"I'm confused," she says, pressing a finger between her eyebrows and studying me. "You want people to think you're settling down with a woman, but you don't want a woman who intends to settle down? How will that work?"

"I want a woman who will *pretend* to want to settle down."

"Okay. I have those connections, too."

"I don't want your damn connections, Sabrina, I want you!"

I take a deep breath, trying to rein in my temper. She's controlling the situation, and it pisses me off. My first instinct is to flip the tables on her, because it's what we do—battle for control, even if it means taking the other person out at the knees, so to speak.

But, much as it pains me, I need her help more than I need to get the upper hand, so I clench a fist and force myself to answer patiently. *Honestly.* "You make me crazy, but I trust you. *Only* you."

I hold my breath, willing her not to flay me into pieces for putting that out there.

There's a long pause as she watches me with an unreadable expression.

"Then trust me to find someone *else*," she finally replies.

I let out the breath I was holding. *Shit.*

Though . . . I narrow my eyes, because there's something just beyond the usual stubborn determinedness in her eyes. Something . . .

She starts to move away, and I grab her arm as I realize what that something is. "You're *scared*."

Sabrina scoffs. "Of what?"

I have no idea, but I do know her well enough to know what'll spur her into action—the action I want.

I lean forward slightly. "You're terrified that you can't do it. That you can't pretend we're a couple without wanting it for real."

This time I get a snort. "Reverse psychology? Really?"

I give her a slow, taunting smile. "Prove it. Prove that you're not completely terrified you'll fall in love with me."

"Oh my God," she says on a laugh, tugging her arm free. "That's *so* not going to work on me."

I shrug, letting my expression go deliberately skeptical as I sip my drink.

The silence stretches on, and she lets out an indignant huff. "You're not that irresistible, you know. This whole *I can't break the little lady's heart* routine is a bit nauseating."

I ignore this and go to her fridge, even though I'm not hungry. "Got anything to eat?"

Exactly as I expect, Sabrina stomps toward me, slaps her palm against the fridge door, and glares up at me. "You're the last person I'd ever fall in love with."

"Have you ever been in love?" I ask, a little curious.

"Of course not," she says.

"You don't believe in it?"

She bites her lip, as though unsure of her response. "Not lasting romantic love like you see in the movies, no."

"Excellent."

"Why is that excellent?"

"Because it means there should be no problem with you posing as my girlfriend."

She laughs a little and rests the side of her head against the fridge. "You're relentless."

"And you're stubborn. Seriously, though . . . What are you so afraid of?" I ask it quietly.

For a moment, her expression's unreadable. Then she gives a slow smile and leans in slightly. "You know, for someone so decidedly anti-relationship, you're pretty obsessed with the idea of my falling for you."

She's clearly not going to answer my question, and I shove aside my disappointment. Figuring out what the hell makes Sabrina tick was never going to be easy. I've always known that.

"What can I say, the apocalypse fascinates me." I lean a shoulder against the fridge, mirroring her posture.

"At least you acknowledge that it'll be the end of the world before I feel anything other than tolerant loathing for you."

"Or I you," I say, lifting my glass in a toast.

She clinks her glass to mine, even as she frowns, a tiny line appearing between her dark eyebrows. "You really think I can't do it? Spend a month as your companion without falling all over myself?"

I push away from the refrigerator and go to the counter, setting aside my drink. "Doesn't matter what I think."

She follows me, touching my arm. "Could you do it?"

"Do what?"

"Spend an entire month in my company without falling for my charms." She says it mockingly, but the question is clearly a challenge.

I've never been good at backing down from a challenge, and one issued by her? Forget it.

"I think I'd manage."

"You know," she says, studying my face, "you've got me thinking."

"Dangerous," I mutter.

"Perhaps this could be good for us."

My heart tightens in my chest as I realize that she's actually considering going along with my plan. "Yeah?"

Sabrina nods. "This weird thing between us . . . the fact that we can't coexist without tearing each other down or tearing off each other's clothes—"

"For the record, I'm always a fan of the last one."

She gives a slight smile. "Yes, but it's not . . . healthy. It's hard on our friends; it's hard on *us*."

"And you think our spending time together will fix that?" I ask, careful to keep the skepticism out of my voice. The last thing I want to do is dissuade her from helping me, but I can't imagine a world where Sabrina Cross and I can go longer than an hour without easing the ever-present sexual tension between us, either by fighting or by screwing.

"I think it will," she says, smiling as she sips her drink. "Pretending to be an item in public could teach us how to be civil to each other, and the near-constant proximity will definitely cure me of my ill-advised attraction to you."

I frown. Even though I sense I'm about to get my way, I'm not at all sure I like where she's headed with this.

Still, I'm a desperate man. "Does this mean you'll do it?"

"On one condition."

"Name it," I say, my pulse thrumming with the promise of victory I sense on the horizon.

She looks at me. "No more hookups."

"No other women until after the Wolfe Gala. Got it."

"No, I mean *we* no longer hook up," she says, using her glass to gesture between us. "We do this, we keep it clean. Literally. I won't be your fake girlfriend *and* your enemy with benefits."

I *hate* this idea. I hate it hard.

Sabrina and I don't sleep together often. Self-preservation and all that. But the thought of never being able to give in to the urge, never to get my hands on her . . .

"One or the other, Cannon," she says quietly. "You can have me pose as your girlfriend, or you can keep me as your occasional booty call."

"Booty call my ass," I mutter. "You initiate those interactions just as often as I do."

"Well I won't anymore. Not as long as we're pretending to be in love." She flutters her eyelashes at me.

"It's a dumb-ass rule," I say. "If we're going to go through this hell together, we might as well get some pleasure out of it."

She shrugs. "Take it or leave it. Of course, there can be casual touches to convince the skeptical public that we're a thing. But in private, hands to ourselves. That's the deal."

I study her perfect features and contemplate. "So I can't touch you, and I can't touch anyone else. Does it go both ways? No guys on the side for you, either?"

She hesitates for a fraction of a second, with only Juno's gentle snores from the dog bed in the corner to punctuate the silence. "Sure. That's fair. No other guys."

Fuck. Fuck me. Because that, right there, is what sells me.

More than my reputation, more than my job, I'm going to agree to this because it means that for a month, I'll be free from the image of other men touching this woman. I'll be able to pretend, even if it really is pretending, that she's mine.

Only mine.

I lift my glass. "It's a deal."

She blinks in surprise but recovers, lifting her glass as well. "Fine. Good."

We lock eyes as we clink glasses, and I realize that I've been wrong. I've been thinking the hardest part of this whole thing will be faking being in love when I don't even believe in love.

Now I know better.

The hardest thing is going to be keeping my hands off the only woman I've ever wanted.

6

Sabrina

Saturday Morning, September 23

When I step out of my apartment building onto Park Avenue, I have two thoughts.

First observation: fall is truly here, and like any proper New Yorker, I smile at the realization, because it means the debut of my new black V-neck sweater, skinny jeans, and suede ankle boots is warranted.

Second observation: Matt Cannon is standing outside my apartment building, leaning back against the window as he waits for me, two Starbucks cups in hand.

His sunglasses block his eyes, but I feel his gaze drift over me as he walks my way. "Morning."

"Really," I say, accepting the cup he hands out. "This is how it's going to be? You just show up whenever you want, no warning?"

He grins. "You're on my payroll now, right?"

"If you're asking if I got the signed contract you sent over yesterday, yes. But if you refer to our arrangement as me being on your payroll again, I'll show you exactly where you can shove the contract."

"You're snippy in the morning. I'd forgotten that," he says, falling into step beside me. "So. Where're we going?"

I take a sip of the drink, unsurprised to find that it's a cappuccino, one packet of raw sugar, exactly as I like it.

Wordlessly I reach out, take his cup from his hand, and sip that.

Pumpkin spice. Huh. Didn't see that coming.

"We're sharing drinks now?" he asks as I hand it back.

"We're a couple, right? What's yours is mine."

Actually, it has nothing to do with that. You know how I said I know everything about everybody? Every now and then, there's a stumper. Matt Cannon's coffee choice is one of them. I've never found the guy to get the same coffee beverage twice.

I know what Ian drinks—Americano with a splash of two-percent in the morning, sometimes opting for something cold and sweet on a summer afternoon. I know what Kennedy Dawson drinks—black coffee, always.

But Matt? He changes.

Sometimes it's a caramel Frappuccino. Sometimes it's a tall drip. Sometimes it's a white mocha with extra chocolate. Sometimes it's a double-shot espresso with no sweetener whatsoever.

Today, apparently, it's a pumpkin spice latte. Tomorrow, who knows? I don't even know why I care. I guess I've always hated things I can't predict, *especially* as they relate to Matt Cannon.

"You didn't answer. Where're we heading?"

I cut a glance at him as I head in the direction of Madison Avenue. "You did see section 7B, right? The one that says all public appearances together necessitate twenty-four-hours' notice?"

"No problem," he says. "Here's your twenty-four-hours' notice that we have brunch reservations tomorrow."

"Let me guess. Are they at some see-and-be-seen restaurant in the West Village that charges twelve dollars for an egg?"

"Twenty dollars if you want to add freshly shaved truffles."

"I'll do that, since you're buying. But that's tomorrow. I didn't have you on my schedule for today."

"You won't even know I'm here," he says.

I snort as we turn onto Madison Avenue, one of my favorite shopping meccas, alongside Fifth Avenue and SoHo.

"Just go about your business. I'll follow at a respectful distance."

"And make sure people see us together?"

"Exactly," he says with a quick grin.

"All right," I murmur, taking another sip of my cappuccino. "But remember, Cannon, you asked for this."

"Asked for what?" he says, automatically opening the door of the store I've stopped in front of.

Instead of answering him, I step inside, waiting until he's followed me inside before glancing around for my usual salesperson.

"Sabrina! Hi. You got my message! I've been holding some of our fall stuff for you. Can I get a room set up?"

"Absolutely, I want to try *all* of it."

I hide a smile when Matt lets out a tiny groan.

He's shoved his sunglasses to the top of his head, and he's looking around the store in that wary way men have when shopping is on the horizon.

Monica gives him a curious look, and I tug him forward.

"Monica, this is Matt Cannon. Matt, Monica has the best damn fashion sense in Manhattan and is largely responsible for making me look reasonably put together on a regular basis."

"Oh please, I could dress you in a bag and you'd look fabulous," Monica says to me as she extends a hand to Matt.

He gives it a quick shake. "Pleasure."

"So, Mr. Cannon, are you just keeping Sabrina company, or can I talk you into trying on a few of our new menswear pieces?"

Matt opens his mouth, no doubt to protest, but I answer first.

"Oh, I've been *dying* to get him into a cashmere sweater," I say, rubbing my hand over his biceps in a way that lets Monica, and anyone else who might be watching, know just what we are to each other without having to utter the word *boyfriend*.

"Absolutely," Monica says, nodding enthusiastically. "I have a bunch of things in mind. Give me a few minutes, and I'll get two rooms ready."

"Fantastic," Matt mutters as he drains his coffee.

I pinch his arm, reminding him of what we're doing here. In turn, he drapes an arm over my shoulder, squeezing just a little too hard in retaliation, though any bystanders wouldn't know it by the adoring smile he gives me.

I give him a glowing smile right back. "How much are you wishing you would have checked with me before tagging along today?"

"Almost as much as I wish this coffee was of the Irish variety."

"You're in luck," I say, finishing the last of my cappuccino before nodding at another salesperson approaching with two glasses of champagne. "It's not whiskey, but . . ."

"It'll do," Matt says eagerly.

"Can I take those coffee cups for you?" the woman asks with a bright smile.

We exchange our Starbucks for the champagne, and I scan the room as I take a sip. This is one of my favorite retailers, and since this is their flagship store, it's extra lavish, as the complimentary champagne would indicate.

Instead of cramming every spare space with tables and mannequins and merchandise, Max & Belle has created a place intended for lingering, with plenty of plush seating and iPads with home screens set to the latest catalog. There are a few standing racks with samples of each item, but the majority of the inventory is kept out of sight, adding to the impression that each item is one of a kind.

"How long you gonna be?" Matt asks. "I can wait outside."

"Monica's bringing you stuff to try on."

"I don't want to try shit on. I have plenty of clothes."

"You have plenty of suits," I correct. "Sweaters, though?"

"I've got some of those, too. I pay a personal shopper an obscene amount of money so I don't have to endure this."

"*Endure?* Yeah, because sipping Veuve Clicquot with Michael Bublé playing in the background while waiting for someone to bring you clothes is a *really* tough life."

"Spare me the pretentious guilt trip. You realize that most people don't count shopping as work, right?"

I turn toward him and lower my voice. "You're the one who wanted to tag along, so we may as well get some use out of your crashing my shopping day."

"How the hell is this going to help my—"

"Matthew. Be quiet and trust me. For the next five minutes, you need to forget that you're pissy about shopping and pretend to be completely smitten."

"Smitten with what?"

I exhale through my nose. "With me, you jackass."

I turn around casually, noting the well-dressed woman on the far side of the shop. She hasn't seen me, but I saw her the moment we entered.

She's the reason we're here.

Time to test Matt Cannon's acting abilities.

I amble to a center rack with a cold shoulder dress, feigning interest in the gray fabric as I let my gaze scan the room until it lands on the woman in the jeans and red sweater, my eyes going wide as though just seeing her.

"Georgie?" I say, raising my voice slightly to get her attention.

The woman spins around, a wide smile on her face. "Sabrina. Hi, it's been forever!"

I walk toward her, and though we do the air-kiss thing, it's the genuine *good to see you* kind, not the vapid-socialite variety.

"You look amazing," I say, pulling back and giving her a once-over.

That, too, is genuine. Her long reddish-brown hair falls to her waist in carefree curls, her sweater fitted to a figure that's healthy without being gym-rat toned, her smile bright and cheerful.

Georgiana Watkins—wait, no, Georgiana Mulroney now—is one of my favorite people in the city. She's sort of right out of a scene from *Gossip Girl* but in the best way possible. She's rich, yes, but also sweet. Relentlessly happy, but in a charming way, not annoying.

"I forgot we both work with Monica," she says, squeezing my hand. "I came in looking for a pair of black pants, but after trying everything on, I'll have, like, eight bags. Marly too," she says, pointing to her BFF, who's chatting on her cell a few feet away.

I give Marly a friendly wave, and she finger-wiggles back and blows me a kiss.

"You just get here?" Georgie asks.

"Yup, me and—" I glance over my shoulder. "Matt, babe. Come over here a sec!" I call.

His eyes narrow just briefly, and I give him a *this is what you're paying me for* smile in return.

"Georgie, do you know Matt Cannon?" I ask, setting my arm on his biceps as he approaches, letting my fingers linger, as though I can't help myself from touching him. "Matt, this is Georgiana Mulroney."

She laughs. "Wow, nearly a year after the wedding, and it's still weird to hear that as my last name. Weird in a wonderful way," she chirps as she shakes Matt's hand.

"I actually know Georgie through her husband," I explain to Matt. "Andrew and I've done business together."

"I always forget he knew you first!" Georgie says. "Andrew's a divorce attorney," she explains to Matt. "Somehow I manage to love the cynical guy anyway."

"I've heard of him," Matt says with an easy smile, his hand finding my waist in a casual, absentminded sort of touch. "Couple guys in my office have hired him."

Georgie makes a sad noise. "I'm so sorry to hear their marriages didn't work out."

Matt blinks and gives me a quick glance that I'm pretty sure translates to, *Is she for real?*

Yup. That's Georgie for you—an optimist, true-love enthusiast, and so on. But her Pollyanna outlook on life isn't why I sought her out. I need her connections.

Monica approaches from the dressing room area and beckons me forward. "Sorry about that, Sabrina, Mr. Cannon. I have two fitting rooms all set up for you."

"Thanks so much," Matt says with a cheerful grin.

Hmm, maybe the guy's better at this than I expected. His rapid transition from the standard man-hates-shopping routine to the easygoing charmer, determined to please his girlfriend, is convincing as hell.

"I'll get you some champagne refills," Monica says with a smile. "If you guys want to head on back?"

"Absolutely." I turn back to Georgie. "It was so good seeing you, hon. We should do dinner soon."

"I'd love that. I'll text you some dates."

"Perfect."

"Okay, so . . ." Georgie leans in with a conspiratorial smile and lowers her voice, as her eyes deliberately take in Matt's hand on my waist. "Did I or did I not see you guys here together?"

"You absolutely saw us together," I say with a sly smile.

Georgie winks. "Got it."

There. Right there. *That's* why I sought out Georgie Mulroney. The woman's not a gossip, but she is a part of the gossip chain when I need her to be.

Matt's and my shopping excursion will be all over the social scene rumor circuit by lunch.

She gives me a quick kiss goodbye and waves at Matt. "So nice meeting you. We should all get together sometime!"

"Absolutely, I'd love that," Matt says agreeably.

After waving goodbye to Marly and Georgie, I lead him into the fitting room area. It's coed, and unlike my high school memories of the Gap, the salespeople aren't worried about groping happening in their changing stalls.

Stalls isn't even the right word. There's an entire room, complete with a small love seat, chair, chilled water bottle . . .

Since I know the routine already, I step into the room Monica points me to, listening with a smile as I hear her rattle off a list of twenty items for Matt to try on.

I've got about twenty of my own items to try on, so I kick off my ankle boots to get to work. I pause once I'm down to my bra and underwear, sipping my champagne as I debate between trying on the dresses first or a fabulous tweed skirt with a bit of flounce around the hem to keep it from looking dowdy.

I'm reaching for the skirt when the door to the dressing room opens. I whirl around, expecting it to be Monica entering without realizing I was in here.

It's not Monica.

Matt shuts the door with a quiet *click* that belies the irritation in his gaze. "You planned this."

I take another sip of champagne and try to pretend that my heart's not beating in overdrive at being nearly naked in an enclosed space with him. "Planned what?"

"You knew I'd be waiting outside your apartment today. You knew I'd tag along. You planned everything. Don't deny it."

I roll my eyes and set the champagne aside on the table. "Why would I deny it? This is what you're paying me for."

"So that interaction with that Georgie chick—"

"All planned," I confirm. "Georgiana has her finger on the pulse of New York society, and she's aware of my . . . occupation. She's exactly the person we need to spread the news organically about our relationship— Honestly, Cannon, are you even listening?" I ask in exasperation, since he's clearly checking me out instead of paying attention.

His eyes return to mine. "You should have told me. Let me in on your plan."

"I *did* tell you."

"Yeah, *after* we got here," he says.

"I don't know why you're so irritable about this," I murmur, inspecting one of the dresses on the hanger and ignoring how vulnerable I feel at my near nakedness.

The dress is pulled from my hands and tossed onto the back of a chair, the hanger falling to the floor.

"Let's get one thing straight: I'm not one of your moronic clients to be handled," Matt snaps.

"I know that. But you've got to trust—"

His hand slips around my neck, tilting my face up, and my breath catches. *Damn him.*

"No hookups, remember?"

"I know," he says, resting his forehead against mine. "But I can't *think* when you're dressed like that."

"I'm not really dressed at all," I mutter.

His smile is strained. "Exactly."

I don't reply, but the sound of our breathing says plenty all on its own.

Want.

Need.

I close my eyes and take a deep breath, fighting for self-control. It's *always* been this way around him, which is the very reason I set up my rule in the first place. I may not be a believer in all things lovey-dovey, but even I know that the combination of pretending to be Matt's girlfriend while also sleeping with him is dangerous.

My brain knows this. My body? Wants him. Always.

I'd been so sure that spending more time with him would cure my attraction to him—that being forced to deal with his arrogance on a regular basis as his faux girlfriend, with the constant exposure to all his flaws, would rid me of any desire for the man.

So far . . . *my plan's not working.*

7

MATT

Saturday Morning, September 23

I'm not sure what annoys me more. That Sabrina's been one step ahead of me the entire time, and I didn't have a clue, or the fact that I want her like crazy, even as I know that, too, is probably part of her plan.

Or maybe not, I amend as I study her expression in the mirror's reflection. Five minutes ago, she looked smug as can be after she ensured our "relationship" made it onto the socialite gossip chain.

Now she's both mad and turned on. Probably mad *because* she's turned on.

I can relate.

"Get out." She says the words calmly. All the heat comes from the lethal warning glint in her eyes.

"Okay," I murmur, letting my lips almost touch her ear but not quite. I tell myself to release her. To honor our agreement, but my damn body won't obey.

She hisses out a little breath at the contact, even as she arches toward me, her body belying her words. "Seriously? You can't go one month without sex?"

I grit my teeth in frustration. "You're telling me I'm the only one wanting right now?"

My other hand slides up her waist until my fingers brush the underside of her bra. In response, she bats my hand away, and even in my irritation, I nearly smile, because it's so her. So *us*.

She whirls toward me, and the air all but crackles around us. With anger, with sexual tension, with whatever else is between us, always.

I wish I knew what it was. I'm not sure it has a name. Because even though I know down to my very core I'm not cut out for the monogamous-relationship thing—I don't want a serious girlfriend ever, much less a wife—the woman in front of me is the only one who's ever made me think maybe.

Maybe.

Helpless against the onslaught, I do the only thing I can think of. I kiss her.

My fingers tangle in her hair, and my mouth is urgent as it claims hers.

She stiffens immediately, her hands going to my shoulders, ready to shove me off.

I gentle my touch, even as I ease closer. I let her know that she can step away if she chooses, but I intend to make damn sure she makes another choice.

I kiss the corner of her mouth softly. *Kiss me back.*

My lips drift over her stubborn jaw. *Want me back.*

I feel the moment she capitulates, her small body softening against mine. I pull her closer, my mouth finding hers again . . .

"Sabrina, how's everything fitting?"

Sabrina reels back at the sound of the saleswoman's chipper voice, and she slaps her hand against my mouth, her eyes commanding. *Be quiet.*

"I'm all good, Mon, thanks!" Sabrina says with an equally chipper tone. I'll give her credit—her voice is as smooth and even as it always is. Not easy to ruffle, this one.

Monica, however, doesn't get the hint. "You need another size on anything? I've had a couple people tell me that the off-the-shoulder dress is running a bit snug."

"Haven't gotten to that one yet. I'll let you know," Sabrina says, pressing her palm more firmly against my mouth.

"Isn't that blue turtleneck gorge?" Monica babbles on. "The second I saw it, I knew it would look uh-mazing on you."

"I love it," Sabrina says. "It's definitely going home with me."

I narrow my eyes, because I'm pretty sure she hasn't even seen the shirt yet.

She presses her hand harder against my mouth. *Shut up.*

I smile against her palm.

"Okay, well, I'll leave you to it. Just pop your head out or give a holler if you need more champagne or a different size or anything. Mr. Cannon, how are things going on your side?"

I bite back a laugh, and Sabrina rests her forehead briefly to my shoulder in defeat.

"Any ideas?" I whisper against her fingers.

She lifts her hand, and though I can practically see the wheels turning in her brain, trying to come up with a solution, she knows when she's beat. Sabrina lets out a little sigh and shakes her head.

"Mr. Cannon?" Monica asks again.

I clear my throat, feeling a bit like I did in prep school when Mrs. Gallagher caught me feeling up Jen Fowler in the utility closet. "All good, thanks," I say, not bothering to keep the amusement out of my voice.

There's a moment of confused silence, and I imagine Monica uttering a silent *ohhhhhh* as the situation clicks into place in her mind.

"Okay, great!" she chirps, her voice a full octave higher than before. "I need to run out to the front real quick, but I'll be back in a bit!"

Sabrina and I stay perfectly still until the lingering silence tells us Monica's left the dressing room area.

"Well," Sabrina says in a quiet voice, stepping back. "That was . . . horrifying."

"Come on. You've never hooked up in a dressing room before?"

"Not since I was seventeen and in a mall," she says, pulling a shirt off the stack of clothes to try on and tugging it over her head.

"I like it," I say, nodding at the fitted red top.

"Shut up," she mutters, attempting to detangle her hair from a tag.

"Need a hand?"

"No," she snaps irritably. "I need for you to get out of here and go figure out what of the stuff she brought you you're going to buy. You know what, just buy all of it. It's the least you can do after—"

"After what?" I ask, swatting her hands aside and carefully pulling the dark strands of her silky hair away from the tag at the back of the shirt.

"After we defiled their dressing room."

"Defiled?" I say with a laugh. "It was a kiss. We didn't even get to the good stuff."

"Thank God for that. I nearly violated my own rule." She sounds genuinely horrified by the realization.

I catch her chin with my fingers, studying her face. "When did you turn into such a prude?"

"I'm not a prude; I'm a professional. This may be a game to you, but it's not to me. This is my *job*."

"Are you forgetting why we're here in the first place?" I ask, stepping closer. "For *my* job. And believe me when I say that my career being on the line is just about the only thing that could compel me to come to you for help."

She blinks, and for a split second, I swear I see something other than the usual disdain on her face. Something that looks a bit like hurt. Then she lifts her chin and it's gone.

"Get out. Go back to your dressing room and prepare your credit card for a workout."

"I don't get why you're so pissed about this," I grumble as she tugs on a pair of pants. "Wasn't this the plan? To let people think we're together?"

"The key word there being *plan*," she snaps, buttoning the pants. "We're supposed to *plan* when people see us together, not get caught acting like teenagers."

I grin. "You know the reason I think you're really mad?"

"I'm just about to faint from holding my breath, dying to know."

"You're mad that we got interrupted. You're mad that I only kissed you, that I didn't put my hands all over you." To piss her off, I reach out and play with a strand of her hair.

Sabrina lifts a warning finger. "Touch me one more time, and I'll tear up our contract, leaving you on your own."

I study her for a moment, debating just how serious she is. Best not to risk it.

My hand drops. "All right. You win this one. Get whatever you're going to get," I say, waving a hand at the enormous pile of clothes. "But have Monica send the stuff to your apartment. We're not carrying the bags around with us."

Her eyes narrow. "Excuse me?"

"I don't want to deal with them when we go to lunch."

"Oh." I can tell she hadn't expected me to want to extend our impromptu day date, but she'd never admit it. "Fine. I have reservations at—"

"Not your place," I interrupt. I'm done letting her be in control. "I'll pick the place."

She puts her hands on her hips. "Where are your reservations? Because my place is sure to get us spotted by—"

"Who's paying the bills here, me or you?"

"You, but you're paying me to get the job done, and lunch at Fig & Olive will ensure the right people see us."

"I appreciate your efforts, but I'm not in the mood for fussy food." I jerk open the door to the dressing room, saying, "Cancel those reservations," as I step out.

"Only if you tell me where your reservations are. What if—"

I shut the door on her protest and go to my dressing room, where a pile of untouched clothes awaits.

I pull out my phone to make lunch reservations. Yeah, yeah, whatever. I lied about already having them. Trust me, it was necessary. To have any chance of surviving the next month, I need to get the upper hand.

I hear the neighboring door open as Sabrina calls for Monica in a too-sweet voice.

"What's up?" Monica says, scurrying back into easy speaking distance.

"So somehow I ended up with the sweetest boyfriend on the planet," Sabrina gushes. "He just offered to pay my entire shopping bill today; can you believe it?"

My head snaps up from the restaurant app on my phone. *Uh-oh.*

"He's a keeper!" Monica says, clearly delighted with the turn of events. "So what did we decide on? Let me see the yeses!"

I close my eyes, already knowing what I'm going to end up buying for my "girlfriend."

"You better get us some more champagne," Sabrina says. "Matt's told me to go ahead and buy all of it."

I shake my head as I make reservations for two at a restaurant where the food is mediocre but the drinks are big and strong.

I know, I know, drinking before noon.

But you've met the woman. Can you blame me?

8

Sabrina

Saturday Lunch, September 23

I frown and look up at the sign as Matt holds open the restaurant door for me. "Isn't this a chain?"

"It is."

"But—"

He plants a hand on my back and gently pushes me forward.

I'm fully braced for garish decor, horrible lighting, and the smell of old onion rings. Braced for everything that reminds me of my childhood, of my mom's occasional stints working at dirty, tired restaurants until she'd be inevitably fired . . .

I'm pleasantly surprised.

The lighting's flatteringly dim, and the restaurant seems to be made up of tall black-leathered booths, no red vinyl or paper napkin dispensers in sight. Nothing to trigger my Philly flashbacks.

Matt steers me toward the bar. I let him, mainly because sitting side by side on barstools somehow seems less intimate than sitting across from each other in a booth.

"You know, nobody's going to see us here," I say, sitting down next to him and putting my purse on the stool beside me. The shopping bags—all dozen of them—are being delivered to my apartment, as planned. "It's just tourists on weekends and corporate drones during the week at chain restaurants."

"I know," he grumbles.

"So why are we here?"

"Because I like it," he says.

"Okay, fine, why am *I* here?"

He sighs. "Honestly, I don't know. I didn't think it through. What I *do* know is that I just spent an obscene amount of money buying you clothes with plenty of witnesses. You got your girl to pump our names into the gossip circuit. Tomorrow, we'll suffer through a stuffy brunch with tiny plates of shit like escarole and free-range turkey sausage. So right now, all I want is to sit in relative silence and get an enormous French Dip sandwich, with an even more enormous martini. Okay?"

I purse my lips and consider. "Okay."

His eyes narrow. "That's perhaps the scariest word you've ever said."

"How do you figure?" I say, taking a sip of the water the bartender's just set in front of me.

Matt leans in a bit farther. "How easily you forget that I know you. And I *know* that any time you easily agree to something, hell is sure to follow."

I hide my smile, because damn it . . . he *does* know me. Readily agreeing to something and playing the part of perfect acquiescence has long been key to my strategy of staying one step ahead of anyone and everything that comes my way.

See, the trick to being in control is letting other people think that they are. No one lets their guard down faster than a man or woman who thinks he or she is driving the ship.

Truth be told, though, right now, my "okay" really is just that—an okay.

Matt's not the only one who's tired. Sure, we've been together all of a couple of hours, most of it spent drinking champagne and shopping.

Not exactly a hard day's work.

And yet, it's Matt and me. Which means there's no such thing as easy. I've spent every minute far too aware of him, and don't even get me started on whatever that was in the dressing room.

I refuse to admit, even in my own head, just how close I came to letting that kiss turn into something more. To letting him back me against the wall. To having a quickie in a dressing room, for crying out loud.

It's everything rash and crass that I've spent my adult life trying to avoid. I've gotten to where I am not so much from smarts, or even hard work, but from impulse control. I stay in control, always.

Well, almost *always*. The man sitting next to me is the one exception.

"Something besides water?" the blonde bartender asks with a friendly smile.

Matt nods to me to order first.

"Belvedere martini. Three olives," I say.

"Same," Matt echoes. "But with a twist."

"You got it." The bartender moves away to fetch the vodka.

"Belvedere, huh? Thought you were a Goose girl."

"I'm a vodka girl," I clarify, picking up the menu. "Equal opportunity."

"And here I thought we had nothing in common."

"Having nothing in common's never been our problem," I say as I peruse the salad options. Seared ahi or chicken? Decisions, decisions.

"Yeah? What *is* our problem?" he asks, turning toward me.

I set the menu back on the bar and fold my hands. "Well. Off the top of my head, I'd say it starts with the fact that you're a presumptuous ass, and I'm—"

"A grudge-holding shrew?"

"It's not like I'm holding some imagined slight," I say through gritted teeth.

"No. But you are holding on to something that happened four years ago. That I apologized for about a hundred times."

"I don't want to talk about that."

"See, *that's* our problem," he says, raising his voice slightly. "You never want to talk about it, so here we are, years later, still hating each other's guts."

"Are you forgetting who's currently helping you save your job?"

"Are you forgetting how much fucking money I'm spending to get you to do that?" he snaps back. "You hardly volunteered out of the goodness of your heart."

"I don't have a heart. Weren't you the one who told me that?"

"Jesus," he mutters, dragging his hands over his face. "It never stops with us, does it?"

I don't answer.

The bartender appears with two blissfully large cocktails. "Any food today, or just the drinks?"

Screw the salad. Lettuce isn't going to cut it if I have to fuel up for dealing with this guy. "I'll have the French Dip sandwich," I say. "With fries."

Matt gives me a surprised look. "I'll take the same. Extra horseradish."

"Why are you looking at me like that?" I ask when the bartender takes our menus and leaves.

"Sort of had you pegged for a *salad, dressing on the side* order."

"Yeah, well, fighting with you works up an appetite."

He grins. "You know what else works up an appetite?"

I laugh a little, because his expression is so classically horny dude. "We're not doing that. Have you already forgotten our plan to move away from the fight-and-hookup thing?"

"*Your* plan," he mutters. "I was just fine with how things were."

I sip my drink. "Do you ever think that maybe the reason we are the way we are is because we hooked up too soon?"

"You mean, do I regret sleeping with you the first night I met you? Absolutely not."

"Bet you regret the morning after," I say, giving him a bland look out of the corner of my eye.

He looks back at me. "You already know that I do."

I take another sip of my drink. He's right. I do know that. To give credit where it's due, he did apologize for what he said that morning. And a dozen times after that, too.

Hell, I don't even doubt that he meant the apologies a hell of a lot more than the off-the-cuff insult that landed us in our roles of adversaries in the first place.

So now you're thinking he's right. That I *am* a shrew who holds a grudge.

I'll cop to the first one. I've never pretended to be a nice, sweet type of female.

As for the grudge part, it's not a grudge so much as . . . self-protection. Matt Cannon hurt me that morning in a way I've always promised myself I could never be hurt.

I have no intention of letting it happen again. I'd rather be angry than hurt, and though he may not even realize it, I think Matt feels the same.

"Okay, let's talk business," I say, popping an olive in my mouth. "Setting the foundation is good, but I can't imagine The Sams are reading *Page Six* or clubbing with Georgie and crew. We're planting seeds to make this whole thing believable, but how do we get to the people who matter?"

"You mean the clients who are threatening to leave because they don't like how I spend my weekends?" he growls into his martini.

"These people aren't trusting you with their piggy bank, Cannon. You're handling millions on a daily basis. They don't have any insight into what your life looks like, except what they saw in the *Wall Street*

Journal. No one wants to imagine the guy in that picture as the one holding the keys to their retirement."

"I'm not sure they want the guy who makes his credit card sweat buying clothes for his 'girlfriend,' either."

I pat his arm with a smile. "I'll take it all back tomorrow if it's going to break your budget."

He clinks his glass to mine in a toast. "Don't worry about it. I can afford it, and it was worth every penny knowing you'll think of me each time you get dressed. Or undressed."

My smile slips, and his grows. "Well played," I mutter.

"I thought so," he says with a wink. "Okay, so about this gala I'll need you to accompany me to . . . It's a big fancy fund-raiser—"

"I've been to the Wolfe Gala before, Matt."

"Sure. As Ian's date."

"As Ian's *friend*," I correct, even though I shouldn't have to. Matt of all people knows that Ian's and my relationship is, and always has been, completely platonic.

"Well this year, you'll go with me. As my girlfriend."

"*Fake* girlfriend," I clarify, moving my drink out of the way to make room for the sandwiches the bartender's setting in front of us.

"Right. If we don't kill each other before then," Matt mutters, taking an enormous bite of his French Dip.

Yeah, well. There's that.

We both lapse into silence, and I've got a feeling the train of his thoughts is probably pretty close to my own:

How the hell is this going to work?

How can we pretend to be in love when we can barely stand to be in the same room together? I'd been so sure that the forced proximity would change things between us, but so far, our relationship feels more complicated than ever. God knows my emotions feel . . . jumbled. And I hate that. I hate that it—

"This isn't going to work," Matt says, interrupting my thoughts.

My stomach drops at his words, though I don't know whether it's the blow to my professional pride or the personal implications. "What do you mean?"

He pushes away his plate, wipes his mouth. "We drive each other crazy."

"You knew that when you asked me to help you," I point out.

"Momentary lapse. I forgot how frustrating you can be."

"*Me?!* You're the one who—" I take a breath for patience, determined not to let him get under my skin. "It's the first day. There were bound to be some hiccups and arguments, given our history."

Matt gives me a curious look. "I'm giving you an out. Why are you not taking it?"

It's a good question. I should take the out. I should remove us both from this situation before things go to hell, but . . .

The thought of failure tastes bitter. I've built my entire self-worth on my ability to control every situation. To *fix* every situation.

I won't let him take that away from me.

"You hired me to do a job," I say quietly. "Let me do it."

"So that's all this is about? Our contract?" he asks, his gaze holding mine.

I hesitate only a split second before nodding, but I can see from the way his eyes narrow that he saw the hesitation. That he suspects this is about more than my job. More than *his* job.

Still, he merely nods in agreement, not pressing me for answers that neither one of us is ready for.

9

Matt

Sunday Brunch, September 24

You know what's a pretty fantastic plan?

Scheduling your "see and be seen" brunch at your bosses' favorite restaurant, in hopes you might bump into them and show off your new "girlfriend."

The second I walk into Rosemary's, I know my plan's about to pay off, because who's sitting at the bar? Sam and Samantha Wolfe, next to Adam Feinstein, an eccentric billionaire known for being old-school with his money strategy.

Granted, this isn't exactly how I thought it would go. I'd deliberately booked an earlier-than-usual brunch and then purposefully arrived well ahead of the reservation, before Sabrina.

My plan was to ensure I got a table by the door, so that if and when The Sams arrived, I'd be positioned in a very cozy, very visible, romantic brunch with my "girlfriend."

But . . . this can work, too. Or at least, I'm determined to *make* it work.

I check in with the hostess, knowing full well that since I'm early, my table won't be ready yet. She assures me that my table should be available "closer to my reservation time" if I want to wait at the bar. Which I absolutely do.

The Sams and Adam are sipping mimosas, likely waiting for their own table, and haven't seen me yet.

I approach, clamping my hand on Sam's shoulder, confident smile already in place. "Mr. Wolfe?"

"Matt!" Sam turns toward me, his expression torn between surprise and wariness. Once again, I feel the intense urge to pummel the jackass who wrote that article and turned my once golden name into the wild card that embarrasses the bosses. "What are you doing here?"

I grin. "It's Rosemary's. I'm doing what everyone does. Getting a damn good brunch."

"Their bread alone is to die for," Samantha agrees, her voice warmer than her husband's, though her expression is no less leery. "Matt, do you know Mr. Feinstein?" She gestures to the other man, who's been more interested in his phone than our conversation about the bread.

Adam Feinstein looks up, shoving his round glasses farther up his nose as he gives me a bland, indifferent smile.

I extend a hand. "Mr. Feinstein, a pleasure. I'm Matt Cannon. I work for Wolfe Investments."

"I know who you are," the other man says, turning his attention back to his phone. "The kid from the *Journal*." He shakes his silver head without bothering to look up. "In my day, people were more careful with their money and reputation. And more *respectful* of other people's money and their company's reputation."

I tense, and Samantha closes her eyes briefly in dismay.

Shit. *Shit!*

As I'm trying to find a respectful rejoinder to Feinstein's clear disdain, I hear a feminine voice saying my name. "Matt?"

Oh thank God. Sabrina has shown up early, bless her.

I turn toward the voice, only I realize too late that the voice is too high to be Sabrina's, and find not one but two blonde women grinning at me.

I've slept with them. *Both* of them. Not at the same time, but I'm guessing that distinction is going to do little to save my ass at this point.

"Hi . . ." My brain searches for their names. Either of their names. I've got nothing. In my defense, it's been years. And though my hazy memory tells me I met them at the same bar, I had no idea that they knew each other, much less were brunch buddies.

They're both looking at me expectantly, and the alarm bells in my head are in full siren mode now, especially when I hear Feinstein sniff behind me, all the judgment in the world infused into the tiny sound.

I hear Sam sigh, and one of the blondes takes pity on me, though not in a way that's remotely helpful.

"It's Kara, silly!" she says, stepping toward me and wrapping an arm around my neck.

My options aren't good. I can let my arms dangle . . . awkward. I can push her away . . . rude. I *can* hug her back . . .

I go with this one, my arm sliding around her waist and giving what I hope is a friendly, platonic squeeze in greeting. "Of course."

I start to pull back, or at least try to, but she clings, turning toward my bosses and Adam Feinstein and, in a scene right out of my nightmares, keeps speaking.

"How do you guys know Matt?"

Samantha's smile is tight. "We work together."

"They're my bosses," I'm quick to add, hoping it'll cue Kara in to shutting her mouth or at least filtering what she says next.

No such luck.

"Oh, how cool!" Kara gushes. "Matt and I use to party together. Oh my gosh, I'm being so rude." Kara pulls back, belatedly remembering her companion. "Guys, this is my friend Robin."

Robin's smile is as tight as Samantha's. "Matt and I have met."

Kara looks at her friend in surprise, then up at me, her expression visibly cooling as she puts the pieces together.

Come on, ladies. It's been years, and we slept together once. Surely neither of them has been holding on to the delusion that we were exclusive . . .

I resist the urge to tug at the collar of my shirt as it suddenly occurs to me that my reputation is in so much more need of rehab than I ever realized.

I try to pull my arm away from Kara under the guise of looking at my watch. "You know, if you'll all excuse me, I'm actually meeting someone—"

"There you are!"

I never thought Sabrina Cross's sultry voice could cause anything other than agitation and arousal, but today, the sound of her low alto brings something else:

Relief.

I turn toward her, but before I can figure out how to explain the mess I've gotten myself into and subtly beg for help, she's taken control of the situation.

With a friendly smile, she touches Robin's arm. "Hi, are you Kara?"

"No, *she* is," Robin says with a stiff nod toward her friend.

"Ah, well, the hostess has been looking for you," Sabrina says. Then she lowers her voice. "I'd get on it if I were you. I've found this place will only hold your reservations for a hot minute before clearing you off the list for walk-ins."

"Oh, okay. Thanks," Robin says, looking at the hostess, then at her friend. "Kara. Let's go."

Kara reluctantly releases my arm, and the second she does, Sabrina's there, somehow nudging the other woman aside without actually touching her. After a last backward glance my way, Kara follows her friend to the waiting hostess.

Just like that, the first of my problems is handled.

"So sorry I'm late," Sabrina says, running an arm intimately over my biceps, then lifting to brush her lips over mine. "I couldn't get a cab for the life of me—" Sabrina breaks off, as though just registering we're not alone. "Oh my gosh! Samantha. Sam. How *are* you guys?"

She moves past me, doing a smooth air-kiss exchange with Samantha, smiling broadly at Sam.

"I haven't seen you since . . . Oh, what fund-raiser was that? Well, it doesn't matter. So wonderful to see you both."

She keeps chatting on, somehow managing to be captivating not annoying, and I practically see the ice melt off the higher-ups, their shoulders relaxing.

"Thanks so much for that book recommendation," Samantha is telling Sabrina. "My book club deemed it the best one we've read all year and absolutely insisted you consider joining our group."

The thought of Sabrina and my boss's boss in a book club together is mildly terrifying, but I'm too relieved to be anything but grateful at the ease with which Sabrina's handled The Sams.

Adam Feinstein is probably a lost cause, but . . .

Sabrina lets out a little gasp of pleasure. "Mr. Feinstein, is that you?" She taps her hand against the man's knee as he sits on the barstool, the gesture playful and familiar.

I brace, expecting him to glower at her, but instead he's grinning broadly.

"Look at you, sitting all quiet in the corner," she says, leaning in to peck his cheek. "Does Geraldine know you're brunching without her?"

Geraldine? Who the hell is Geraldine?

Feinstein adjusts his glasses with a smile. "She's visiting her sister in Fort Lauderdale this weekend. The Sams were kind enough to let me be a third wheel."

"And Amy?" Sabrina asks. "How's she liking Harvard?"

"Nothing but happy phone calls these first few weeks," Mr. Feinstein says proudly. "We couldn't be prouder, and also, more grateful. Without you making that phone call . . ."

"Oh stop," Sabrina says with a wave of her hand. "Amy's brilliant. I'm sure she'd have gotten into Harvard without my help."

My head is spinning. Sabrina knows Adam Feinstein? And his wife? And helped his daughter get into Harvard?

"You're here with, ah—" Adam looks at me, as though he either can't remember my name or doesn't want to remember it.

"You've met Matt, right? Matt Cannon?" She moves back to my side and makes a big show of rolling her eyes. "I can't say I'm loving how well everyone knows his name these days. Bachelor parties—every woman's worst nightmare, right?"

She gives a playful wink at Samantha, and the CEO doesn't miss a beat. "Let's just say I'm grateful Sam's bachelor party days are behind him. I don't have to worry about him getting into too much trouble anymore."

Sam clamps my shoulder with fatherlike affection and leans in. "Had myself a lap dance or two in my day. Is it just me, or are those women persistent? Never could figure out how to get out of the situation without being rude."

The hostess appears with three menus. "Wolfe, party of three? Your table is ready. I apologize for the wait. The party at your table decided to order dessert at the last minute."

"A decision I can get behind," Mr. Feinstein says, standing and picking up the fedora he left on the bar. "I might go for some dessert myself. Sabrina, sweetheart, it was so good to see you. Geraldine will be upset she missed you."

Sabrina pats his hand with a smile. "We'll have to get together when she gets back from Florida. Cocktails?"

"That'd be great." Mr. Feinstein's gaze is less fatherly when he looks at me but a good deal friendlier than before. "Mr. Cannon, good to meet you. You'd best stay out of trouble if you're going to be worthy of this one." He hitches a thumb at Sabrina.

"Absolutely, sir. Lesson learned."

The man smiles and pats my arm with a nod.

The Wolfes give me a meaningful look that says we'll talk later before we all say our goodbyes, the three of them following the hostess toward the back of the restaurant.

Sabrina takes the barstool vacated by Feinstein and, catching the bartender's eye, orders two mimosas before crossing her legs and turning to face me with a triumphant smile. No doubt about it, she knows that she skillfully unfucked my entire morning and did it well.

Damn it. There'll be no living with her now.

10

Matt

Sunday Brunch, September 24

"Why aren't you gloating?"

Sabrina sips her mimosa. "Why would I gloat?"

"Because you know full well that you saved my ass."

She shrugs. "That's what you're paying me for. I don't need to gloat. I already know I'm good at what I do."

"Yes, you are. I . . . underestimated you. I apologize."

She gives me a startled look, then studies me, as though looking for sarcasm. She can look all she wants; there is none. I can give credit when it's due, and it's definitely due here.

We've been seated at our table for nearly half an hour, and every moment that passes, my tension eases a little bit more. While I'm not out of the woods as far as my reputation goes, I'm confident I made a solid step forward in the damage-control department, thanks to her.

"Are they watching us?" I ask.

"Can't tell," Sabrina says. "But just in case . . ." She scoops up a forkful of eggs and holds it across the table for me, an adoring smile on her face.

I roll my eyes, something I can get away with, since my back is to the Wolfes and Feinstein.

Still, I dutifully eat the eggs off her fork, because apparently, that's what people in love do? I wouldn't know.

"You think he bought it?" I ask.

"Who, Adam?" she asks before taking another sip of her mimosa.

I shake my head at her casual use of his first name. "Yeah, *Adam*. How is it you've never mentioned you're on a first-name, best-friend level with Adam Feinstein? And his wife? And his daughter?"

"This is why you're paying me the big bucks," she says with a smile. "And they're a sweet family. They invited me to a Hanukkah party last year."

"You celebrate *holidays* with them? You're not even Jewish."

She shrugs. "So? They know that. Just like they know the holidays can be lonely."

I look up at that, a little startled by the admission. For some reason, it never occurred to me that someone as sassy and confident as Sabrina Cross would ever be lonely, but . . .

Of course she would be. How could she not be? My family drives me up the fucking wall, but it's still a warm place to go during the holidays, where they're happy to see me.

I don't know the details of Sabrina's family situation beyond the fact that she has none. Or at least none she keeps in contact with.

My throat tightens with guilt at never having thought to include her in any holiday festivities. Not that she'd have taken me up on the offer, but thinking of her spending them all alone . . .

"Quit looking at me like that," she says, nibbling on a piece of bacon.

"Like what?"

"Like you feel sorry for me. I assure you, I'm just fine with my holiday routine."

I want to ask more about it. If she celebrates alone. Or with Ian. Or . . .

"Your bunnies just left," she says, derailing my thoughts.

"My bunnies?"

"The bar bunnies: Kara and Robin."

I wince. "Right. In my defense—"

She holds up her hands. "Don't. You don't owe me explanations, remember? And I'm sure there's a perfectly reasonable defense for how you can't be bothered to remember the names of women you—"

I reach across the table and stuff some of my Benedict into her yapping mouth.

"Sorry," I say as she chews, glaring all the while. "Thought I saw Feinstein coming this way. Wanted him to know how besotted I was by sharing my food."

She swallows and opens her mouth.

"And," I say before she can speak, "I knew their names at the time. It's just . . . been a while. I mean, what are the chances that two women I haven't slept with in years not only know each other but also show up today, in the same restaurant?"

"It's a popular brunch spot," she says, lifting her shoulders. "I know half the people here."

"Yeah, I figured that out. We can't seem to go five minutes without someone stopping by to schmooze with you."

"Which is working in your favor." She points her mimosa at me. "The more people who see us together, the better."

"I know."

She leans forward. "Why do you look so tense? It's just brunch. Don't you like brunch?"

"Not really."

"Everyone likes brunch."

"No, not everyone likes brunch. I hate all the fanfare. Why can't we just get a pile of eggs and be done with it?"

She lifts her eyebrows. "A pile of eggs?"

"You know what I mean." I push my plate aside. "Brunch is always such a fucking production."

"You're getting pretty pissed about a meal, Cannon. You're still on edge?"

"Yeah, I guess," I admit. I thought my tension was gone, but perhaps it's only eased. I still feel . . . off. "My plan of showing up where I suspected The Sams would be came dangerously close to backfiring."

"Yes, well, that's why we should follow *my* plans. But regardless, I think I dug you out of that pile of crap quite nicely. Though, to be honest, I don't see Adam giving you his business. He's very old-fashioned."

"That's fine," I say, taking a sip of mimosa. "I don't want him as a client."

"No?"

I shake my head. "The Sams have been after him for weeks, but if they get him, Kennedy's got dibs. It's a good fit. The two of them can discuss chess strategy or whatever."

Truth be told, I love chess. And I'm damn good at it. But I don't get off on the dignity of the game or whatever, like Kennedy does.

"Yeah, that makes sense," she says thoughtfully. "If nothing else, Kennedy would probably go crazy for the Feinsteins' first-edition Dickens collection."

Snore.

"Also, he just left."

"Who?"

"Adam."

"Thank God," I say, exhaling. "I feel like I've been on display. The Sams didn't leave with him?"

She shakes her head, glancing over my shoulder toward their table. "No, it's just the two of them."

"Probably trying to figure out which one has to fire me."

"I don't think so," Sabrina murmurs, still watching the older couple. "They seem sort of . . . romantic. She's feeding him a bite of something chocolate, and he just wiped a bit of powdered sugar from her lip."

"Blech."

"I think it's sort of sweet."

I give her a sharp look, surprised to see a wistful expression on her face. "Wait." I lean forward. "I thought you didn't believe in the whole romance thing."

She shrugs. "I don't, not really. Not in the sense that I think there's one person who completes each of us or that romantic love is reliable."

"Right," I say with a nod. "Marriage is crap."

"No, I don't think so," she says.

"Right, and—Wait. What?"

"I don't think marriage is crap," she repeats.

"You just said—"

"I said I think fairy-tale versions of marriage are crap," she clarifies. "But with the right mind-set, I think marriage can be . . . nice. In its way."

"You want to get married?" I say, jarred to my core.

"I don't know. Maybe. Someday. Yeah, I think so," she says, seeming to warm to the idea. "With someone who was on the same page as me about it."

"What page is that?"

She bites her lip and thinks it over. "Well, I don't want a big white wedding, with the whole *to love and to cherish* bit. But I don't necessarily want to spend the rest of my life alone, either. It'd be nice to have someone to share my life with. A companion."

"You have Juno."

The soft expression on Sabrina's face fades at my glib tone. "Never mind."

"Sorry," I say, meaning it. "That was a dick thing to say. I'm just surprised. I thought . . ."

"Thought you and I were both cynics?" she says with a small smile.

"We are. I'm just saying, in theory, I could see the appeal of having a partner. Someone to come home to, someone to talk to about my day. Someone to have dinner with."

"Someone to go to brunch with," I supply.

"Right. Exactly."

Our gazes lock and hold, and something strange passes between us.

"But you don't like brunch," she says on a rush.

"Right. No. Definitely not."

"Good," she says.

"Great."

We resume our meal in silence, and though she turns the conversation back to my "reputation rehab" and her suggested plan for the upcoming week, I have a hard time keeping my attention on the topic at hand.

All I can think about is Sabrina and her idea of marriage as a partnership of sorts. And how if and when she finds that partner, it'll mean the end of meals like this one.

The end of *us*. Whatever we are.

11

Matt

Monday Afternoon, September 25

It's been a day for distractions. Alarm didn't go off. Spilled coffee on my shirt. Couldn't get a cab. Lost another client. Worked through lunch.

It's not even five o'clock yet, and the day's not done with me. The distraction currently headed my way is perhaps the worst yet. Or at least the most annoying.

Unfortunately, it's also unavoidable.

I pick up my phone. "Hey, Mom."

"Hi, honey!"

My mom's always pretty cheerful, but the borderline manic happiness in her tone confirms she's calling for the reason I'd suspected.

She's heard the news.

"How are you?" she asks, her voice too casual.

I sigh and lean back in my chair, rubbing my forehead. "Well, shitty, actually. The whole Vegas thing isn't dying down as readily as I hoped it would."

"Oh, it will," she says breezily.

I clench my teeth against irritation. My parents had called, separately, the day the *Wall Street Journal* news broke last week. And though there'd been the token concern and sympathy, my mom hadn't wanted to discuss the topic for longer than two minutes.

She's a nice enough woman, but she tends to determinedly ignore anything she deems unpleasant that doesn't impact her directly. So I know she's not calling to check up on that bit of news. She's calling about the other news.

"How was brunch yesterday?" she asks in a gleeful, teasing tone.

Yeah. There it is.

Besides getting the face time I'd hoped for with my bosses, Sabrina predicted our see-and-be-seen brunch date yesterday would result in plenty of press. Not quite *Wall Street Journal*–level press, but it had gotten picked up on enough society blogs that I figured my mom would have heard about it through her vast gossip circuit. My parents live in Connecticut, but my dad was a Wall Street guy, so they're still pretty plugged into the scene. *My* scene. Lucky me.

"Brunch was fine."

"Looked a bit better than fine. You were feeding her, Matthew."

Only to shut her up.

"She's gorgeous," my mom gushes. "Sabrina, was it?"

I give a grim smile. "Like you haven't already googled everything about her."

"There's not much," my mom says with a touch of sulkiness. "Her social media accounts are private, and though she's connected to plenty of powerful people, I couldn't find any information about her."

Exactly as Sabrina likes it.

"She's private."

"Well. Whatever. You looked happy."

I grimace. "How many pictures were there?"

"Just a couple. But I could tell by the way you looked at her that you're crazy about her."

I roll my eyes.

"Is she the one?" my mom asks with the slightly desperate tone of a woman who, by her estimation, is long past due for grandchildren.

The fact that my mom thinks there's ever going to be "the one" is laughable. Though I wouldn't hurt her by telling her outright, she and my father are pretty much solely responsible for my skepticism on all things monogamy and happy relationships. A lifetime of seeing just how jacked up marriage is will cure a guy of any happily-ever-after delusions pretty quickly.

"We're just dating, Mom." *And not even for real.*

"How'd you meet?" she asks.

"She's a friend of Ian's. They grew up together."

"Oh, that's nice."

I grunt in response, and she sighs. "I can see I'm not going to learn any more from you than I did from the internet."

"Yeah, well, I don't think grown men typically give their mothers details on their love life."

"I know that," she says pragmatically. "Which is why I need to get the details from *her*."

I've just put my feet up on my desk, but they drop back to the floor. "What?"

"This woman. Sabrina. I want to meet her."

"No," I say automatically.

"Why not?" she says in a pouty voice.

"Because we've just started dating. I'm not going to freak her out by bringing her to my parents' house."

Not that I can ever imagine Sabrina freaking out about anything, but then, she doesn't know the debacle that is my home life. A glittery, white-fence facade hiding a rotten core.

"Dinner. This weekend," she pushes.

"I'll come to dinner," I agree, knowing I'm past due for a visit. "But I'm not bringing Sabrina."

She huffs. "Matthew."

"Mother."

"Think about it?"

I hear a knock at the door, and I look up in relief when I see Ian standing there, eyebrows lifted in question. I gesture him in.

"Mom, I gotta go. I have a meeting."

"Okay, honey. I'll see you next week with Sabrina. I love you!"

"I'll see you next week. No Sabrina. Love you, too." I hang up to end the debate and toss the phone on my desk.

"No Sabrina where?" Ian asks.

"My mother heard we're 'dating' and wants me to bring her to dinner."

Ian snorts. "Now that, I'd love to see. Sabrina playing your doting girlfriend at your perfect parents' house."

I look away, a little stab of guilt kicking in that I hide the truth about my parents even from my best friends.

"How's the Sabrina thing been going?" Ian asks.

I run a hand over my face. "I'm exhausted."

"It's only been two days."

"Yeah, well . . . let's just say if being her fake boyfriend is this exhausting, I pity the guy who will take on the role for real someday."

Pity and hate.

"Not happening," Ian says emphatically.

I drop my hand. "No?"

Ian shrugs. "Sabrina's more relationship averse than you."

Huh. Interesting. Interesting that Sabrina's never mentioned her unique thoughts on marriage to her best friend.

Still, it's not my place to spill her secrets. Plus, honestly? A tiny part of me is thrilled that I know something about her that Ian doesn't. The two of them have always been thick as thieves.

"She is a bit cynical about romance," I say evasively. "But she's never said why."

Ian gives me a look. "Yeah, I'm not walking into that one. If she wants you to know what makes her tick, she'll tell you herself. And don't scowl at me. You know I'd protect your privacy just as much if she asked me about you."

"Does she?"

Ian laughs. "Really? Here. Distract yourself with this." He shoves forward a fancily wrapped gift that's just been placed on my desk.

"What is it?" I ask.

"A present."

"I see that. Why is it on my desk?"

"What's wrong with you? I think the words you're looking for are 'thank you.'"

"I'm not going to say thank you until I know what it is and what it's for."

I start to reach for it, but Ian shakes his head and drops into the chair opposite me. "Actually no, not yet. Have to wait for Kennedy."

"Dude. Why are you being weird?" I ask, noticing he has another matching gift in his hand. Had I not been so distracted with my mother's call about Sabrina, I'd have noticed them before. In my defense, the packages are small.

"For the record, none of this was my idea," he mutters, looking uncharacteristically embarrassed.

A moment later, Kennedy ambles in, most of his attention on his cell phone. He sets it aside as he sits next to Ian. "What's up?"

"Ian brought us presents," I say.

"It's not my birthday," Kennedy says. "Nor is it yours."

"Thank God we waited for him," I say to Ian. "How else would we ever keep track of everyone's birthdays?"

Kennedy reaches out and pulls the gift from Ian's hand. Sniffs it.

Ian rubs his forehead. "Oh my God, what are you doing?"

"I was just making sure it wasn't incense," Kennedy says.

Ian gives him an incredulous look. "Why would I be buying you incense?"

"Last gift I got was sandalwood incense."

"You need new friends," I tell him.

"It was a housewarming gift from my mother."

"You ever use it?" Ian asks curiously.

"Sure. It's right next to my collection of scented candles and face creams." Kennedy holds up the sleek gift. "Now stop stalling."

Ian sighs. "Okay, well, it's like I told Matt—this wasn't my idea, and . . . Shit. You know what, just open them. Get it over with."

Kennedy and I exchange curious glances as we untie the silver ribbon and tear open the black paper.

"Now, see, this is already much better than incense," Kennedy says, sounding a bit more cheerful than before as he opens the box.

"Agreed," I say, pulling the metal hip flask out of my box. "Dude, did you fill it?"

Ian nods. "Vodka for you, scotch for Kennedy. That much, at least, was my idea."

"Explain."

Ian blows out a breath. He scratches his ear.

I narrow my eyes. "You're stalling again."

"Yeah, well, give me a break; I've never done this before," he mutters, shifting in his chair.

Kennedy unscrews the top of his flask and extends it to Ian. "Here. This'll help."

Ian laughs. "I'm more of a gin guy, but . . . sure, what the hell."

He takes a sip, then hands the flask back to Kennedy. Meanwhile, I'm turning my own flask over, trying to figure out what sort of metal it's made out of, when I notice the inscription.

It's dated for February of next year.

I look up. "Dude. Isn't that your—"

"Wedding date. Yeah," Ian says. "I need a best man. Well, men. You guys are it."

Ah, shit. I don't think of myself as a sappy kind of guy, but the request means a lot. Well . . . it was more of a demand, but still.

"I sort of thought this was unnecessary," Ian continues. "I mean, I figured you guys would just know, like, the moment we got engaged. But Lara said I had to make it official . . ."

Grinning, I stand and go to give my friend a hug. "Hell yes, man. I'm going to look so much better in a pink dress than Kennedy."

"You jest, but Lara is thinking pink and red for our colors. It's Valentine's Day weekend, blah blah blah."

"I'm not wearing a pink tie," Kennedy says, giving Ian a hug of his own. "Red, we can talk about."

"I'll pass on the message."

"You know, you didn't have to bribe us," I say, nodding toward the flask.

"Lara's idea. Apparently, you can't just ask your wedding party to stand up beside you anymore. It has to be a thing. Can someone please change the subject?"

He sounds desperate, so Kennedy takes pity on him and turns to me. "How'd it go when you ambushed Sabrina on Saturday? Was she pissed?"

I groan. "It backfired. The infernal woman knew I was coming, flipped the tables, controlled the entire day."

Well, not the entire day. There'd been a moment in the dressing room when she'd been dangerously, wonderfully close to being out of control.

"She's good at that," Ian says in acknowledgment before looking at his watch. "Damn it. I've got to run. Drinks later on me as a thank-you for not giving me shit about the dippy best-man gesture?"

"Oh, there will be shit-giving," Kennedy says. "We just haven't gotten around to it yet."

"Fantastic. Can't wait," Ian says. "But just keep in mind that I have an excellent memory. And I'll remember each and every bit of shit-giving you dish out when it's your turn to walk down the aisle and your fiancées make you beg me to be your best man with a cupcake or a poem."

Kennedy winces. "Noted. I'd like to think it won't go down that way, but if a woman ever winds me around her finger to propose, she can probably convince me to do just about anything."

"It'll happen," Ian says, clamping Kennedy on the shoulder as they head out the door. "You too, Cannon."

I smile confidently as I sit back at my desk, because no matter how determined Ian is to bring me down into his lovestruck world, I know I'll never join him there.

I don't do love. I don't do relationships.

And I sure as hell never plan to do marriage. Not the drippy, delusional love version.

And not Sabrina's way, either.

12

Sabrina

Monday Dinner, September 25

I blink in surprise. "Are you wearing an apron?"

Lara McKenzie points a wooden spoon at me in warning. "Definitely. Wouldn't you if you were attempting to make dinner wearing a white shirt?"

"Well, see, that's the difference between us," I say, stepping into her apartment and shutting the door. "I wouldn't be making dinner."

"Yeah, I'm not so good at it myself, but I'm trying. Ooh, but you made dessert!" Lara says, looking down at the apple tart in my hand.

"Nope. Bought it. It's better this way, trust me."

"Are you one of those women who keeps shoes in her oven?" Lara asks as I follow her into the kitchen.

"Not anymore. But when I first moved to the city and was living in a four-hundred-square-foot shoebox while trying to get my business off the ground? Damn straight."

"Now that's something I'd kill to see," Lara says, giving the sautéing mushrooms a quick shove with her spoon. "Baby Sabrina."

"I was nineteen."

Lara shoots me a smile over her shoulder. "Like I said. Baby."

I smile back, though I don't know that I agree. I suppose for some people, nineteen is just another shade of youth. For people like Lara, even Ian, whose paths had involved a four-year university, theirs had held youthful experiences like dorm rooms, study groups, frat parties.

At nineteen, I'd already been putting food on my own table for a decade. I'd learned way more than I should have about the masochistic nature of men, and I sure as hell knew that the only person you could count on—really count on—was yourself.

Even Ian, who'd been my friend and protector since we were kids, had left. I didn't resent him for following his dreams to Yale. I'd been his biggest cheerleader. But my happiness for him didn't take away the fact that I'd really, truly been on my own, all before my twentieth birthday.

Don't feel sorry for me. I don't feel sorry for me. The tough knocks early on gave me my independence, and I'm grateful. Really.

"Can I help?" I ask Lara as she shoves back a strand of hair that's come loose from her pony and peers at an open recipe book.

Lara's one of those women who looks as gorgeous polished and badass in her FBI power suits as she does in jeans and a T-shirt.

She looks up and pushes her black-rim glasses higher on her nose. "Pour us some wine?"

"On it." I go to the fridge. "Ooh, champagne. *Nice* champagne. What are we celebrating?"

Lara gives me an enigmatic smile. "You'll find out when Kate gets here."

I give her a curious look. "Within the past year, you landed your dream job and your dream man. What else could possibly—" My eyes go wide. "Are you pregnant?"

"What?" she squeaks. "No! Would I have bought champagne if I were pregnant? God. Don't do that. Pour me a glass of the Sauvignon Blanc as punishment for giving me a heart attack."

I pour us each a glass of wine and continue to study her. "What, then?"

"Nope." She sips the wine. "I told you, we have to wait for Kate."

I sigh. "I hate waiting." Still, I settle onto a barstool with my wine as Lara begins chopping an onion.

I've been to this apartment dozens of times over the years, settled on this very barstool, but always as Ian's place.

Now it's Ian and Lara's, and it's perfect.

I turn in my chair, scanning the room, smiling a little as I see that it's both the same as I've always remembered and yet . . . happier. The furniture's still classic dude, all black leather and practical coffee table. But there are bits of Lara here and there. A fuzzy blanket on the back of the couch I've never seen before. Cheerful yellow flowers on the bar cart. Black stilettos kicked into the corner.

"*Soooooo*, how was brunch yesterday?" Lara asks me, setting her knife aside and taking another sip of wine.

I spread my arms to the side. "I'm alive, so . . . better than expected."

"Yes, but is Matt?" Lara asks.

"He's fine. I went easy on him."

Lara's head tilts. "You're handling this whole thing better than I thought."

"I know, right?"

She gives me a look. "You think it means something?"

"Do I think what means something?"

"Don't play dumb," she says bluntly. "Is there something there?"

"It's not like we're holding hands and having a sing-along in the streets. We're merely tolerating each other."

"Oh, come on." She sulks. "Give me *something*."

I eye her suspiciously. "Are you going to take whatever I say right back to Ian?"

"Not if you don't want me to," Lara says.

I look away so she doesn't see how much the simple statement means. I always knew the time would come when I'd lose my best friend to the love of his life. Well, not *lose* him . . . but you know how it is. It's always hard on friendships when both people are single and then one of them enters into a serious relationship. Schedules change, patterns shift. It's even trickier when it's best friends of the opposite sex.

And though technically things aren't exactly as they were—he tells Lara things before he tells me—I've gained more than I've lost. Instead of losing a friend (Ian), I gained a new one (Lara). And it's not just a token "play nice" sort of friendliness when the three of us are in the same room.

Case in point? Tonight's a girls-only night. Ian's been banished to who knows where . . . probably to Matt's or Kennedy's. It's just Lara, Kate, and me.

And yup, that would be Kate Henley, Ian, Matt, and Kennedy's assistant. Also known as one of my favorite people on the planet.

The doorbell rings, and Lara holds up a finger. "Don't think you're off the hook. You're not leaving tonight without giving us a full rundown on you and Matt."

She goes to the door and opens it for Kate, who's got a baguette balanced across the serving dish in her hands. "Ugh, so sorry. Of course it's the girl on appetizer duty who's late. Are you guys starving?"

I lift my glass. "Grapes."

"Perfect. I'll take a fruit serving as well," Kate says, marching into Lara and Ian's kitchen like she owns it. "You need the oven for a few?" she asks Lara.

"Nope."

Kate punches some buttons and sets the foil-covered baking dish inside the oven. "The artichoke dip needs fifteen minutes or so to heat. Sorry again about being late. I thought I had all the ingredients, but then I was out of salt of all things, so I had to make a last-minute store run—"

"Stop apologizing," I say, pouring a glass of wine for Kate and setting it beside the cutting board she's pulled out to begin slicing bread.

"Do you know what Lara's news is? She wouldn't tell me until you got here."

Kate practically drops the bread knife she's just picked up. "News? What news?"

I laugh at the surprised irritation on her face. "*Whaaaaat?* Is it possible there is crucial information that Kate Henley wasn't the first to know?"

As assistant to not one but three top Wolfe guys, Kate's one of those people who's always one step ahead of everyone.

Everyone except Lara, apparently.

"It's my job to know stuff," Kate says primly. "And you're no slouch in the reconnaissance department, either."

I clink my glass to hers. "Too true. Because knowing stuff is also my job."

Not in the same way, of course. The type of information Kate gathers is information she'll need to keep Kennedy, Matt, and Ian out of trouble and doing their job. The information I deal in is the kind you lock in safety deposit boxes while making a half dozen thumb-drive backups.

"Hey, knowing stuff is my job, too!" Lara chimes in. "Do you think that's why we've all become friends?"

"No," Kate says pragmatically, resuming her cutting. "Because you entered our circle thinking that Ian was guilty of insider trading. *That* went well."

Lara points her spoon at Kate in warning. "My job was to investigate *if* he was guilty."

"Old news. I demand a subject change," I command, going back to my barstool perch.

"Oh, FBI Lady over there knows I've long forgiven her," Kate says, blowing Lara a kiss. "I mean if Ian can sleep with the woman who almost put him in jail, I can have dinner with her."

Lara rolls her eyes but smiles as she sets her wooden spoon aside. "Okay, active prep's done. The sauce just needs to simmer for a while."

"What are we having?" Kate asks.

"Sautéed chicken breast with some sort of mushroom sauce," Lara says, waving at a cookbook. "My mother swears it's foolproof, and since she's not exactly Martha Stewart, I trust her."

"Lucky," Kate says, shoving a piece of bread in her mouth. "My mom makes Julia Child look like a slacker. Homemade *everything*. I thought she was going to disown me when she learned I didn't make my own chicken stock."

Lara glances at me over the top of her wineglass and opens her mouth, then shuts it again and looks away.

I swallow, because I know she was about to include me in the mom conversation but thought better of it. I'm not sure what Ian's told her about my history, but none of it would be good. And though my first instinct is to stay silent, to keep that shit locked in the vault, I find a rare urge to share.

To let someone in just a tiny bit.

I take a sip of my wine for courage. "My mom once handed me a ten-dollar bill and told me it was food money for my two half brothers and me. I thought she meant while she went out that night. She came back four days later."

Kate and Lara both stare at me for a moment, then Kate shakes her head. "Damn. You win."

I let out a relieved laugh that I don't have to deflect any pity, just good old-fashioned *that-sucks* sentiment. Because it had sucked. "I totally win."

"Did she ever get her act together?" Lara asks, leaning on the counter as Kate checks her dip in the oven.

I shrug as a way of evading. "I left when I was nineteen, as soon as my half brothers were under custody of relatives on their father's side. The few times that we talk on the phone, she invariably hangs up on me."

Lara's blue eyes flash in anger. "Her loss."

I look down at my wine, then back at Kate. "Is it hot yet?"

"Nearly," Kate says, shoving the rack back in the oven. "How about we go to the living room and hear Lara's news?"

I know what she's doing, and I give her a grateful look. It was hard enough to even mention my mom. I definitely don't want to get into a big old thing about it.

Kate gives a quick nod in acknowledgment, her dark-brown eyes conveying understanding.

Kate and I are just about as different as can be. My eyes are blue to her brown. I'm five seven; she's five one. We've both got brown hair, but she wears hers in a blunt shoulder-length cut, frequently pushed back with a slim headband. Mine is halfway down my back, and its tousled style requires thirty minutes with two different-sized curling irons every morning.

She had a modest, conservative upbringing in southern New Jersey with a kindergarten-teacher mom and a mathematician dad. I grew up in Philly's worst neighborhood with a mother who most of the time was so drunk she didn't even remember she was a mother. She was certainly never a mom. My father? Dead of an overdose before my first birthday.

The rest of my mom's men were hardly the "father figure" variety. I learned that the first time one of her boyfriends bought me a bikini from Kmart in January and suggested I try it on for him. I'd said no, and my mom had screamed at me. I was thirteen.

But backgrounds aside, Kate and I both grew up into the same type of person. Strong, smart, and completely unwilling to buy into the idea that our lives would somehow be more complete with a man in it.

That said, I'm pretty damn sure Kate Henley's hopelessly in love with Kennedy Dawson. Not that he knows it.

I'm not even sure *she* knows it.

"Sabrina, can you grab some champagne flutes?" Lara says, gesturing toward a cabinet. "I know we still have some white, but we'll just have to double-fist for a while."

"Don't have to twist my arm," Kate says, going into the living room and flopping onto the couch. "Man, I love this view."

"Isn't it about the same as your view from the office?" Lara asks, pulling the champagne from the fridge and joining Kate in the living room.

Kate snorts. "Yeah. Because my seven a.m. to seven p.m. nonstop schedule *really* allows for admiring the office view."

"Well, you're welcome here anytime," Lara says.

"You hear that, Sabrina?" Kate says with a playful grin at me as I walk toward them. "We can come watch Lara and Ian be disgustingly in love anytime!"

"Hey!" Lara exclaims.

"Oh, come on, honey," I say gently, setting the glasses on the table in front of us. "It is a little like every day is Valentine's Day around here."

"I know," Lara says with a happy sigh. "Maybe after the wedding it'll stop feeling like a fairy tale."

"I doubt it," Kate says. "I've seen the way Ian looks at you. I've never seen anything quite like it."

Hmm. Was that the tiniest trace of longing I heard in Kate's voice?

Or worse . . . was it my own heart giving a quick squeeze at the thought of having someone care about me—*for* me—the way that Ian loves Lara?

"Okay, so what's your news? I want that champagne already!" I say, beyond ready to be done with the sentimental part of our girls' night.

"Well, we can't open it yet," Lara says, taking a breath. "See, I hope my news is good, but I won't really know until I hear your responses."

"Get to it already," Kate demands.

Lara balances the Dom Pérignon bottle on her knees, rolling it slightly between her palms, and I realize she's nervous.

"Okay, so you guys know Gabby," she says on a rush.

"Padilla, Gabby. Your best friend, former roomie. Model. Lives in Paris with her boyfriend," Kate recites automatically.

"Yes, thank you," Lara says in an amused voice. "Anyway, Gabby's agreed to be my maid of honor, and I'm thrilled. But I'm also a little bummed, because other than the bachelorette party, my bridal shower, and the actual wedding, I know it'll be hard for her to make it back here for stuff. I know I haven't known you two long, but . . ." Lara takes a deep breath. "You're some of Ian's closest friends, you've become my closest friends in the city, and I'd love it, really love it, if you'd be bridesmaids."

There's a long moment of silence as Kate and I sit there slightly stunned.

Kate recovers faster than I do. "Hell yes," she says, her face breaking out into a huge grin. "I'd be honored. I'll even wear an ugly bridesmaid dress, because that's what friends do. Now open that champagne and let's talk venue, because I've got a whole list of reception locations. Have you considered a boat? Because a chartered yacht could really—"

"Whoa, hold up," Lara says with a laugh. "We've barely decided on the date!"

I notice she doesn't look at me, and I appreciate it. Somehow, she knows that I need a minute, because . . .

Damn it. *Damn it.*

It takes me a second to even register what's happening, because I'm so not a crier, but . . . yup. There are definitely tears stinging the corners of my eyes.

"Yes," I blurt out. "Absolutely."

Lara's expression erupts into a happy smile, but Kate's look is downright puzzled. "Sabrina, are you—"

"Shut up," I say with a laugh, dabbing at my eyes. "And Lara, you're lucky you've become one of my closest friends, too, otherwise I'd never forgive you for ruining my makeup."

Lara's response is the pop of the champagne cork. "Now we can enjoy this."

"So where do we start with the planning?" I say, accepting the flute she hands me.

"Oh, who cares about that right now?" Lara says, lifting her glass in a toast. "I'm the bride-to-be; I get to decide what we talk about. And right now, I want to toast to the possibility that Matt and Sabrina are finally on the verge of coming to grips with their thing."

My head snaps up in surprise. Whoa, hey. How the heck did this become about me?

"I'll drink to that. The sexual tension between those two has been suffocating me for years," Kate says, lifting her glass. "Sabrina? Ready to spill your guts?"

"No," I grumble. But then I stand and lift my glass to theirs anyway.

I don't believe in love—but I *do* believe in friendship.

And these girls right here are as good as it gets.

13

Matt

Tuesday Midday, September 26

"Jacket on, Cannon, let's go."

I'm not sure how long it takes my brain to register the interruption. I've been told it's a full minute until I shift from Calculator Matt to Human Matt.

It's always been that way, though luckily my colleagues at Wolfe Investments are a good deal more understanding than the jerks in fourth grade who'd been less than impressed by my early ability to do complex equations.

I don't need to do math in my head as much anymore—my job's more about intuition and research than it is actual number crunching. But it still feels like there are two parts of my brain at work when I review a portfolio: the part that's processing the trends, the word on the street, that particular client's financial goals, and the computer part, as I use to think of it, that can't see a set of numbers without processing them endlessly.

My assistant's used to my process more than most, so after barking her initial order to get my jacket, she remains still, waiting for Human Me to catch up.

"What?" I finally say.

She points at the suit jacket I've hung on the back of my chair. "Put that on."

Other than glancing at the clock, I don't move. Unless I've got an in-person meeting, I don't wear my suit jacket in the office. And my sleeves are rolled up to my elbows more often than not. I like to be comfortable when I work. Or as comfortable as I can be in a career where suit-and-tie's basically an official uniform.

"You have a lunch appointment."

I frown. Admittedly I'm awful at managing my calendar, but I'm at least adept at reading the damn thing. And there was no lunch meeting when I checked it that morning.

"It's just a conference call with—"

"Nope, I rescheduled that," Kate says.

I narrow my eyes, because though I trust my assistant implicitly, rarely does she change my schedule without telling me first. It means something's up.

She glances over her shoulder, then goes to close the door before returning to my desk and sitting in the chair across from me.

"The Sams have lunch at Nobu today."

"So?" I can't imagine why I would possibly care that Wolfe's CEOs are having sushi for lunch.

"They're not going alone. Jarod Lanham is joining them."

That gets my attention. Jarod Lanham is one of the world's most famous billionaires. American by birth, he's been a resident of Monaco for the past decade or so. The man's only thirty-six, but already rumors of his net worth hover in the nine-billion range.

In other words, exactly the client Wolfe and every other company on Wall Street would kill to have. Not just because of the sheer amount of money, but his relative youth means that it could be both a profitable relationship and a long-standing one.

I want him. Everyone wants him, but I really want him on my list. I've been following him for years, impressed by his investments, his ability to steadily amass wealth even as he dominates the social scene in every country he visits.

In other words, Jarod Lanham is me but on the other side of the accounts. A fellow "boy wonder," so to speak.

Kate knows my obsession. So do The Sams.

"They didn't invite me," I mutter, standing and unrolling my shirtsleeves. Even after Sabrina saved the brunch situation on Sunday, they've been keeping their distance.

"Can you blame them?" she says. "You're persona non grata around here. They already have an uphill battle to impress Lanham with Ian's scandal being so fresh."

I nod. I understand, even though it sucks. This should be a pivot point in my career, and instead of having the opportunity to convince Lanham I'm his guy, I'm sitting idly by while everyone mistakenly assumes I spend my weekends cock-deep in cocaine and hookers.

"I got you a table," she says as I button the sleeves. "And I think I sweet-talked the hostess into getting you into the same part of the dining room as The Sams, but she couldn't promise anything."

"She sound like the bribing type?" I ask with a grin. Movie cliché as it may seem, slipping a hundred or more to a maître d' is hardly unheard of around this part of town.

"No, she sounded young and flirty."

My grin widens. "Say no more."

Kate sighs impatiently. "Matt. That was your old reputation. If you go around flirting with a nineteen-year-old hostess, you'll confirm what everyone thinks of you. Which would be an especially awful idea today."

Something in her tone gives me pause. "Why especially today?"

Kate smiles smugly. "I called Sabrina."

I freeze in the process of reaching for my jacket. "What?"

"This is what you're paying her for. We need people to think you're dating her seriously, but more important, we need the *right* people to think that. The whole reason you're doing this is to convince people like Jarod Lanham that you're stable and trustworthy. You need her there."

I groan.

Kate tilts her head. "Why are you so resistant? Isn't this the plan?"

I shove my hand through the sleeve of my jacket with less care than the expensive garment deserves. "I'm not resistant."

Kate crosses her arms. "Yes, you are. Spill."

"We're not talking about this," I mutter, heading toward the door.

Hell, I don't even want to *think* about this. I don't want to think about the fact that my stomach knotted at the thought of seeing Sabrina, not because of hate, not even because of want, but because after last weekend . . .

I worry I could start to enjoy her. Enjoy *us*.

To an extent I've always enjoyed what we have—the bickering, the sex. *Definitely* the sex.

But this past weekend, even around the frustration and exhaustion, there was something else there. Potential. Potential that the two of us share something deeper.

Sure, she wants me dead. And there were a handful of times I'd have happily strangled her. But counterintuitively, there was a strange easiness between us, too. Almost as though our mutual wariness of the other person and romantic entanglements frees us up to be our true selves. With each other.

I'm annoyed she's coming to lunch. Not because I don't want her there.

But because I do.

Makes sense, right? *Crap.*

"She'll meet you there," Kate says bossily, following me down the hallway toward the elevators. "Your reservations are at noon under your name. The Sams and Lanham have twelve thirty reservations, so your being at the same restaurant should seem coincidental instead of desperate stalker."

I punch the elevator button and look down at her. "How the hell do you know these things? Not only that he's in town and having lunch but also the when and where?"

She smiles. "As if I'd reveal my methods."

"You're damn good at your job," I say as the elevator doors open.

"I know."

I step inside and turn to face her. "I'm grateful."

Kate rolls her eyes. "I know that, too."

"Anything you don't know?" I ask with a grin.

"What happened with you and Sabrina all those years ago?" she says hopefully.

My smile drops, and the elevator doors close, saving me from responding. As if I could.

I'm not sure *I* even know what happened.

14

Sabrina

Tuesday Midday, September 26

"You're late," I say, not glancing up from my phone as Matt comes through the front door of the restaurant.

"Does anybody like you?" he mutters irritably, crossing his arms as he stands in front of me.

I grin. "Lara does. She asked me to be a bridesmaid." I can't help it. Two days later, I'm still riding high on that one.

His gaze searches my face, and when he smiles back, I have the strange sense he gets what the invitation meant to me. "Yeah?"

"Yup."

His smile gets wider. "Excellent. I'm one of the best men. Maybe we can walk down the aisle together."

I purse my lips. "Actually, now that you mention it, it's a church wedding. I'm *pretty* sure your skin will burn off if you try to enter the building."

"Ha-ha," he says drily. "Shall we?" He puts a hand at the small of my back and nudges me toward the desk.

Matt checks in with the hostess, who motions for us to follow her.

He extends a hand, gesturing for me to precede him. *Amateur.* I ignore this, instead looping my arm in his and tugging him forward.

"Say something charming," I whisper.

"Your ass looks amazing in that dress," he says under his breath.

I let out a low chuckle so that anyone watching assumes we're sharing an intimate inside joke, but my words are chastising. "I said charming not horny."

"Compliments are charming."

"Sure. Compliments on smiles. Hair. A woman's *ass*, not so much. No wonder you're single."

He glances down at me. "I'm not single at the moment. I have you."

I open my mouth, ready to sling back a tart retort, but . . . I don't have one.

I have you.

I know what he means. He's hired me to pretend he's no longer single. But for a moment, the idea that we have each other felt . . . *nice.*

"Thanks for coming today," he says quietly. "I didn't find out about Kate's plan until after she already called you."

I feel oddly disappointed that it was Kate's idea to call and not his.

He puts his lips to my ear. "Say you're welcome."

His proximity sends a quick ripple of awareness down my spine, and the way I lean into him, just slightly, isn't even faked, though I hope like hell *he* won't know that.

"Here we are!" the hostess announces, motioning us toward the center of the room.

It's not a great table, right in the middle of all the foot traffic, but for what we need it for, it's perfect. It'll be impossible to miss Matt's bosses when they come in. Or for them to miss us.

"So what's our play?" I ask, picking up the menu once we're seated. "Cocktail with lunch to signal we're on a midday date or iced tea to show your new responsible side?"

"Cocktail," he mutters. "Definitely cocktail."

I look at him more carefully, taking in the shadows under his eyes, the tension in his shoulders. “You okay?”

“I’m fine. I just want a damn drink. And lucky for me, The Sams are of the *Mad Men* era, three-martini-lunch mind-set,” he says. “They’d be more skeptical if I *wasn’t* drinking.”

I continue to study him. He looks mostly the same as always. Impeccably styled blond hair. Blue eyes that can go from playful to guarded in the span of a single breath. His suit’s a dark navy today, the slim silver tie keeping the look modern and sharp instead of corporate dowdy.

But there’s a restlessness about him, alongside the weariness. Even as he studies the menu, I can tell his brain’s elsewhere.

“You’re nervous,” I say quietly, so none of the neighboring tables can hear.

His eyes snap up. “What would I be nervous about?”

“You tell me.” Normally I’d call him out on his mood swings, but instinct tells me to tread carefully. “This client. He’s important?”

“Kate didn’t tell you who it is?”

I shake my head. “No. Just said that Matt’s ‘girlfriend’ was needed, that it was important.”

“It’s Jarod Lanham.”

I blink. I don’t get starstruck by name-dropping very often, but even I can appreciate the wow factor of one of the world’s most watched billionaires entering the Wall Street sphere. “Well. Crap. He’s like . . . your spirit animal.”

His smile flashes, and I’m relieved to see that it’s a real one.

“You know him?” Matt asks. “Hell, of course you do.”

“No, actually I don’t,” I admit. “He’s not in New York very often, and though we’ve gotten invited to plenty of the same events, both here and in Europe, our paths have never crossed.”

Plus, he’s never needed my services, which is how I make most of my acquaintances.

Our server comes over to ramble about today's raw bar and take our drink order.

"A glass of the Chardonnay, please," I say, following Matt's lead on the boozy lunch.

"Make it a bottle," Matt says, handing over the cocktail menu.

"You hate Chardonnay," I say as the server moves away.

"I don't hate it. I like vodka better, but splitting a bottle of wine's romantic." He looks at me in question. "Isn't it?"

"I suppose," I muse. "Truth be told, I spend a lot of time faking romantic evenings, not a lot of time actually enjoying them."

Matt leans across the table toward me. "I seem to remember an evening four years ago that was romantic, and there was no faking. I don't think."

"That wasn't romantic so much as . . . sexual."

His eyes narrow slightly in challenge, and I get the sense he's calling me a liar.

He'd be right.

That night when Matt and I first met had been romantic. And sexual. Hell, it'd been magical.

In the span of hours, he'd made me feel like no man had in my entire life. Butterflies, breathlessness, the whole bit.

And even though we've let the horrific aftermath of the whole thing determine our current relationship, the truth is, the good stuff is always there, lurking in my subconscious like a cherished memory, perfectly protected.

Matt sets an elbow on the table, palm out, and beckons with his fingers for me to put my hand in his.

I do. We're playing the part of smitten, after all.

And though I know it's pretend, my stomach tightens the second our palms touch. Even more so when he maneuvers so that my hand is cradled in his, his other hand coming up to rest fingers against the center of my palm.

The knot in my stomach tightens. *Want.* And a little bit of fear.

I try to hide both emotions with a coy smile. "Nice move. Setting the scene?"

In response, he drags his fingers lightly along my palm. My breath catches at the caress, but instead of looking smug, he looks intent. Thoughtful as he holds my gaze.

The server appears with the bottle of wine, but instead of releasing me, Matt continues his gentle caress, directing the server to let me be the one to do the tasting.

With my free hand, I taste the wine and declare it perfect, though truth be told, I don't really register the flavor of the Chardonnay. I'm too aware of the man I'm sharing it with.

I clear my throat. "So what's the plan?" I ask. "You're going to just hold my hand until they get here?"

His gaze drops to the spot where his fingers continue their slow caress of my palm, before moving in a teasing circular motion that immediately calls to mind all the places I want his touch.

I try to jerk my hand back, but he holds it firm and looks up to study me. "You're jumpy."

I'm facing the front of the restaurant, and I do a quick scan to ensure Matt's bosses haven't come in yet. There's no sign of them.

"Save your moves for when they're actually here," I say, gently extracting my hand from his.

He lets me go with a thoughtful expression, and it takes all my self-control not to ask what's going through his head. I know how to deal with snarky Matt, charming Matt, even irritable Matt. But this version, the one with the soft eyes and secretive thoughts . . . he throws me off-balance.

I hate being off-balance.

I pick up the menu once more. "Okay, what are we getting? Do you like sushi?"

"Nope. Came to a sushi restaurant but can't stand the stuff," he says sarcastically.

I don't bother to look up. "Yes, well, you came to a restaurant with a woman you can't stand, so you'll excuse me if I don't take your actions at face value."

"Who says I can't stand you?" he asks.

I lift my gaze to his. "Um, you? Every time you look at me, snap at me, pick a fight with me . . ."

"That's a two-way street, Ms. Cross."

"I never said it wasn't."

Matt runs a hand over his face. "I swear to God, talking with you is impossible."

"I'm happy to sit in silence until the show starts."

"I don't—Damn it, I don't want to sit in silence, and I don't want to fight."

I set the menu back on the table with an irritated slap. "Well, it's you and me, so silence and fighting are the only options."

"They don't have to be. If you weren't so damned stubborn—"

My jaw drops. "Do *not* put this on me. I'm here because I signed a contract, and in no part of that contract does it say that we have to like each other. I committed to convincing others that I'm wildly in love with your playboy ways, but don't think for one second—"

"Matt. Sabrina. We certainly seem to have the same taste in restaurants this week."

Matt's heated gaze snaps away from mine as we both look up to see The Sams standing over our table, along with Jarod Lanham, who looks just as put together and appealing in person as he does in pictures.

Matt recovers quickly, standing to greet them. "Nobu is definitely the best cure for sushi cravings."

"Indeed," Samantha says, looking torn between admiration and wariness at the fact that Matt's so clearly manufactured a way for us to end up in their path. *Again.*

I give Matt a quick, deliberately shy look, as though not quite sure how he wants me to handle it, then turn my sheepish smile on them. "You must think I'm the worst influence, dragging him out for a lunch date on a workday."

"Nonsense," Sam says. "I have my heart set on an ice-cold martini myself. Do either of you know Jarod Lanham? Jarod, Matt Cannon's one of our best brokers. This is Sabrina Cross, his . . ."

"Girlfriend," I say with a self-depreciating eye roll. "Don't mind me."

Matt extends a hand to Jarod. "Mr. Lanham. A pleasure."

Jarod Lanham's an attractive man—tall and lean, with a strong jawline to balance out his otherwise narrow features. Dark hair with just the slightest gray at the temples that promises excellent silver-fox potential. And when he smiles, like he's doing now, the laugh lines and straight white teeth flashing against tanned skin make him even more appealing.

"Mr. Cannon." He shakes Matt's hand. "Of *Wall Street Journal* fame."

I keep myself from wincing. Barely. The Sams' poker faces aren't as good. Sam visibly flinches, and Samantha's eyes close in brief exasperation.

Matt's shoulders stiffen slightly, but he keeps his expression friendly and lets out an easy laugh. "Ha, yes. Note to self: check for cameras when attending a bachelor party."

"You should party with me sometime," Jarod says. "No cameras. Plenty of private entertainment."

The billionaire's dark eyes drift my way as he says it, and though I'm braced for a smarmy, smug dismissal, his gaze is frank and assessing.

And appreciative.

I've been around long enough to know when a man likes what he sees, and I've definitely gotten the stamp of approval from Jarod Lanham.

Matt knows it, too, his blue eyes narrowing just slightly. I nearly smile, because I bet in all of Matt's carefully calculated scenarios of how his first meeting with his dream client would go, Jarod admiring his "girlfriend" wasn't part of any of them.

"Ms. Cross. It's a pleasure to finally meet you." He extends a hand.

Finally? He knows me? "Likewise," I say, placing his hand in mine and trying to hide that he's caught me off guard.

"You're a . . . consultant." His eyes lock on mine as he says it. The confidence in his gaze makes me realize he knows full well what I do, but since people don't go around dropping the word *fixer* in meetings like this, he's stuck with my more generic title.

"I am."

He nods. "I'm familiar with your work. I may actually be in the market for your services in the near future, but that's for another time."

I feel a little flutter of surprised pleasure that *the* Jarod Lanham might want to hire me, but I push it aside, remembering that I'm here for Matt.

Jarod glances at our table, the barely touched wine. "If you haven't ordered yet, why don't you join us?" He glances at The Sams. "If that's okay with you."

I press my lips together to hide a smile. Jarod Lanham could have told Sam and Samantha he was bringing a rabid raccoon to lunch, and they'd have put the animal at the head of the table with champagne and caviar.

"Absolutely," Sam says. "Matt's one of our best. I think you'll enjoy talking with him. You know he joined us when he was twenty-two?"

Jarod runs a thumb along his jaw. "That so?"

Samantha turns to the hostess, who's been standing a discreet distance away. "Is a table for five available?"

The woman's eyes widen in panic. "Five? Well . . . I'll have to check. We have a limited number of tables for larger parties, especially during the lunch hour, but, um—"

"Actually," I interrupt. "This is sort of a lifesaver. I had a work issue come up, but I didn't want to leave Matt to eat alone. If you all don't mind my begging off, you'd just need a table for four."

Samantha and the hostess practically sag in relief.

"I hope we're not running you off," Jarod says as I lift my purse from the back of my chair.

"Absolutely not. It's just that duty calls."

"Understood," Jarod says quietly, clearly still assessing me.

I swear I hear Matt let out a faint snort, which reminds me why I'm here in the first place: damage control for Matt's career.

I give Jarod a vague smile in response, and after nodding goodbye to The Sams, I move around the table to Matt. My touch on his upper arm is for the group's benefit.

He leans down to kiss my cheek. "I'm sorry our lunch got cut short."

I blink in surprise at the sincerity in his voice. We both know Jarod Lanham is the goal here, not me.

Don't we?

"Call me later?" I ask him, letting my voice go soft and a little hopeful.

"Of course." His eyes stay locked on mine.

Even when I turn away, I feel his gaze between my shoulder blades. And though I know it's for Jarod's benefit, a part of me wonders—hopes—if his possessiveness isn't so much about saving his professional career as a broker as it is staking his claim. As a *man*.

15

Matt

Tuesday Evening, September 26

"Let me get this straight. You had lunch with Jarod Lanham. And our bosses. Lanham told you he'd be in touch. And you're looking like someone kicked your puppy?"

I glare at Ian. "I don't have a puppy."

"Evading," Kennedy chimes in, pointing at me accusingly. "Ian's right. You're not nearly as happy as you should be."

"I don't have Lanham's business yet. You'll have to excuse me if I'm not popping the champagne."

The guys and I are at one of Wall Street's favorite after-work watering holes, and I'm halfway through what I expect to be the first of many cocktails tonight. And not the celebratory kind.

My friends are right. I should be ecstatic that Jarod didn't laugh me right out of the restaurant. That he knew about my Vegas notoriety and still seemed to entertain the idea of working with me.

Hell, the man ended our lunch meeting with the implication that I was on his short list of potential brokers.

"Lanham say why he's in the market for someone new?" Ian asks. "He's been with Herbert Bishop for a hundred years."

"Precisely. Bishop's practically a hundred years old. He's retiring," I answer.

"So why not stay with Morgan Stanley? Surely Bishop's got a half dozen protégés itching to take over."

"Probably. But the last thing I wanted to do was plant the seed that he should stay where he is. Besides, I got the sense the man thrives on change."

Ian takes a sip of his Negroni, a bitter red gin cocktail he orders wherever he goes. "Wanna flip for him?"

I grin, knowing my friend's joking. "You'll have to pry his billions from my cold, dead fingers."

"Jarod Fucking Lanham." Kennedy shakes his head. "Unbelievable. You realize that you're on the cusp of achieving everything you've ever wanted at twenty-eight. It's hard not to hate you."

I smile reflexively, but I'm taken aback at Kennedy's words: *Everything you've ever wanted.*

Is that right?

Is getting an elusive billionaire client my life's dream? Is it really everything I've ever wanted?

I suppose that's right.

So why do I feel so hollow?

Because Jarod Lanham was looking at Sabrina. And she was looking right back.

Okay, so I'm not entirely sure about the last one. Sabrina had been in her role as my girlfriend, and to give credit where it's due, the woman rivals any Academy Award winner when it comes to her acting skills.

Even I'd have been convinced that she was into me if I didn't know better.

But I'm definitely not imagining that Lanham had been looking at her. And if I know anything about the man from my years of watching him from afar, it's that he gets what he wants.

He'd wanted Sabrina.

I can't blame the man. She'd been sexy as hell in a blue dress that matched her eyes, her hair long and tousled, her heels high and begging to be wrapped around a man's waist . . .

I look up at Ian as I reach for the complimentary nut bowl in the center of our table. "You talk to Sabrina today?"

"No, not in a few days. Why?"

I hate myself for it, but I feel a tiny stab of relief that Sabrina hasn't gone running to Ian to talk about how miserable she is in her and my current arrangement. Though I know her and Ian's relationship has never been romantic or sexual, I'm always . . . aware of it. Aware that she'd do anything for him, whereas she won't do a damn thing for me unless money and an ironclad contract's included.

And no sex.

That part has been worse than I expected. Of course, I've always known how hard it is to be around Sabrina and not touch her. I just figured I'd . . . get over it. I figured that if a line was drawn in the sand, my constant boner for the woman would get over itself.

Not so.

I want her more than ever.

Which, I've been trying to assume, is just the result of the age-old "wanting what I can't have," but I'm terrified it's something worse. Terrified that I want her more *because* I'm spending more time with her. Talking with her. Studying her. Seeing how her brain works.

Everything you've ever wanted . . .

Damn it.

"She's meeting Lara for drinks, though."

I look up at Ian. "What?"

He rolls his eyes at my distractedness. "You asked about Sabrina. I said I hadn't talked to her, but Lara mentioned she and Sabrina were going to grab a drink before dinner."

"When? Where?"

"Never had you pegged for a clingy boyfriend," Kennedy says, snatching the nut bowl away from me. He looks down, then glares at me. "You ate all the almonds and left the shitty peanuts."

"So ask for some more almonds. And I am not a clingy boyfriend. You know we're only—"

"Posing for the people, I know," Kennedy interrupts. "But no need to keep up the pretense for Ian and me."

It's a trap. One of the subtle, barely noticeable verbal traps that Kennedy Dawson is legendary for. Kennedy's got a low, almost monotone voice. He never yells, rarely laughs. All three of us are sarcastic, but Kennedy's humor is dry to the Sahara level.

I'm sure Kennedy and Ian expect me to either deny the comment or jump to reassure them that Sabrina and I still hate each other, that we're just pretending. But I'm feeling ornery, so I surprise them. And myself.

"Lanham wants something from her."

"From who?" Ian asks.

"Sabrina. Keep up, man."

"I thought you said she left lunch as soon as he and The Sams showed up."

"Yeah, but she didn't Irish goodbye. She chatted. Made nice. *Then* excused herself."

"I see," Ian says, grabbing the nut bowl from Kennedy, then setting it aside in disgust when he sees it's empty. "And at what point in this interaction did Lanham slip the note into Sabrina's locker about having a crush on her?"

I point my glass at him. "You don't get to be sarcastic about this. We had to listen to you overanalyze Lara's every blink for months."

"He's got you there," Kennedy tells Ian. But my reprieve is temporary. Kennedy turns back to me. "So what if Lanham likes her. Hell, it could work in your favor."

I'm already shaking my head. "She's supposed to be my girlfriend. Hell, the entire reason for that is so I don't lose out on clients like Lanham because of my wild ways or whatever."

"But you've already got Lanham halfway there," Kennedy points out. "Which means either The Sams overstated the impact of the *WSJ* article, or Lanham doesn't give a shit, or you and Sabrina were damn convincing at lunch and he thinks you're a settled man."

I toss back the rest of my drink. "It's not the last one. Or if it is, he wouldn't hesitate to make a move if given the chance."

"So? Let him. You want Lanham. He wants Sabrina. He'll probably crash and burn with her as every man does. What's the harm in letting him try?"

"Guess we'll find out."

I turn toward Ian. "What?"

"You were so into your ranting, I didn't have the chance to tell you that Lara and Sabrina were meeting here for a drink. I just got a text from Lara that she's running late, but it looks like Sabrina found someone to keep her company while she waits." He nods his chin toward the bar.

My head whips around, and hot possession rips through me.

Sabrina's at the bar, all right, still wearing the sexy blue dress from earlier. Her head tilts back as she laughs at something the man next to her said.

A man who's none other than Jarod Lanham.

16

Sabrina

Tuesday Evening, September 26

So, billionaires can be genuinely charming. Who knew?

Jarod Lanham uses his elbow to indicate my nearly empty drink. "Another?"

I hesitate for a second, and he immediately picks up on it. "I'm being pushy. Forgive me."

"No, it's not that. It's just . . . convenient that you're at the same bar as me, on the same day I met you. I can admire a man with a plan. Just wish I knew your angle."

"No angle. All I want is to buy you another drink." When I narrow my eyes, he gives a sheepish grin. "I suppose that sounded a touch desperate."

I laugh at that. "I don't think anyone could ever describe you as desperate."

He grins and leans forward on the bar. "I confess, the money does help people overlook the flaws."

"Yeah?" I sip the last of my drink. "And what would the flaws be?"

The second the words are out, I blink a little in surprise. *Oh hell.* Was that flirting?

I mean, not that I'm any stranger to flirting—I've practically built a career out of being good at it. But usually it's with an agenda. This had just . . . slipped out.

The bartender comes over, and Jarod gestures for another round for both of us with an assertive spin of his finger.

Instead of using the barstool I'd been saving for Lara, Jarod's leaning against the bar, and he shifts now so he's fully facing me, elbow on the counter.

"My flaws," he says with a smile. "You sure you're ready for them? We've just met."

I make a bring-it gesture with my fingers.

He leans forward slightly. "I can be alarmingly single-minded. When there's something I want . . ." He shrugs. "I get it."

He holds my gaze as he says it, and it doesn't take a genius to figure out what he's saying. Or rather, what he's not saying. Not out loud, anyway.

Still, the guy's perceptive enough to know I was at lunch with Matt, so his forwardness, while flattering, is also a bit off-putting.

"Question," he says, crossing his feet at the ankle. "Your services. You ever help people sort out their personal life?"

I take my time before answering. Normally I'd play coy a bit. Figure out how much he knows about me before confirming *exactly* what it is I do.

But this is Jarod Lanham. He wouldn't waste my time. Or his own.

"What did you have in mind?" I ask.

He looks away, and I'm surprised to see there's a flash of uncertainty there.

"Mr. Lanham. Anything between my clients and me—and that includes potential clients—stays between us."

He fiddles with the cocktail napkin, just for a moment. "I'm, ah—" He clears his throat. "Sort of looking for a . . . matchmaker."

I'm careful to hide my surprise. It's not an uncommon request. I get people asking all the time to fix them up with someone compatible when they don't have the time or inclination to try dating apps or no longer hope to meet someone the old-fashioned way.

But Jarod Lanham is a billionaire. And a good-looking one.

Unless he's got *really* creepy skeletons in his closet, he can have pretty much any woman he wants.

Jarod apparently reads my thoughts, because he gives a derisive laugh. "I know. It sounds ridiculous."

"No. Surprising, maybe, but not ridiculous. Have you been dating long?"

He shrugs. "I've had girlfriends. Some of them serious, but none I can see myself sharing a life with."

"You're looking for a wife," I say, deciding to cut straight to it.

He nods. "Yes. I'm not in a hurry, but I'm also not getting any younger. I've never wanted to be a bachelor forever."

"Understood. I'd be happy to make some time for us to go over what you're looking for."

"I already know exactly what I'm looking for."

I laugh. "All right. Let's hear it."

"I don't want someone fluttery. I'm not looking for some grand love or any of that bullshit. I just want someone to . . . be with."

I swallow, a little alarmed by how closely his sentiments echo what I told Matt at brunch on Sunday. "I see. So you're not looking for a love match."

He shrugs. "I want someone I can trust. Care about. But I don't expect to feel butterflies, nor do I want someone who expects to be swept off her feet." His smile is rueful. "You're probably thinking I sound like an unromantic asshole."

I smile into my drink. "I've heard worse."

"You and Cannon," he says curiously. "You've got the whole thing? The butterflies, the sweeping?"

It's on the tip of my tongue to confess I don't know what Matt and I have. Then I remember my role: *Matt* is my current client, not Jarod.

I get a minute to come up with my answer as the bartender delivers our drinks. Jarod nods in thanks, then turns back to me, expectant but not prying.

"We haven't been dating long," I admit. "But . . ."

"There's something there?"

I allow myself a little smile. "Yeah. Yeah, there's something there."

Don't know what. But it's there.

He studies me. "I think you'd have a good sense of what I'm looking for. In a woman, I mean."

"How soon are you thinking? I'll be honest; I have a waiting list . . ."

"You can't shoot handsome billionaires to the top of the list?" he says with a charming smile.

I laugh. "Not cocky ones, no."

Jarod shrugs. "All right. I can wait."

"Really? You don't strike me as overly patient."

"How do I strike you?" he asks with a flirty grin.

We're interrupted before I have to answer.

"Mr. Lanham. It's good to run into you again."

My head whips around. "Matt?"

Jarod won't know it, but he's about to see exactly how good I am at my job.

I slip immediately into character, pivoting toward Matt with a wide smile on my face. "We were just talking about you."

Matt's looking right at me, and the expression on his face takes me aback a bit. I'd been expecting wariness—I am talking to his chief target after all, the entire reason he needs me to pose as his girlfriend in the first place. But he's beyond wariness. He looks . . . *mad*?

Jarod extends a hand. "I figured I might run into someone I knew here. The Sams mentioned it was one of the popular Wall Street hangouts."

"They'd be right," Matt says, barely disguising the edge in his voice. "Am I interrupting?"

I resist the urge to roll my eyes. This is so not the time for him to play jealous boyfriend.

"Not particularly."

"Good," Matt says decisively. "Have you given any thought to whether or not we might be a good fit?"

"I'm still thinking," Jarod says blandly.

I look between the two of them, a little surprised that their conversation at lunch apparently went so far as to talk specifics. Matt must want this deal *badly*.

"I understand," Matt says. "That said, I also don't like games. If you're not intending to give me your business, I'd prefer to know upfront."

I give myself a quick pat on the back for not laughing out loud. *Don't like games, my ass.* Matt's entire life is a game. So is mine.

Only *this* one we're playing together, which makes it all the more dangerous.

"I said I'm still thinking," Jarod repeats, all but daring Matt to push him further.

Luckily, Matt's smart enough to know when to drop it. He leans in to kiss my cheek, deliberately pressing his lips close to my ear in an unmistakably intimate, *mine* gesture.

I smile and lean up to adjust his tie. "Hey, you found me!"

He smiles back, but his eyes stay cold. "Looks like we crossed wires about where we were meeting. I had a table in the back."

"Oh shoot, sorry!" I say, stepping immediately into the charade that he and I had plans. "I just assumed we'd grab a spot at the bar."

I say a quick prayer of thanks that Lara's in on our arrangement. If she walks in, she'll know better than to blow our cover.

Jarod reaches for his wallet and sets enough money on the bar to cover his and my drinks plus a generous tip. "I know my reputation is ruthless, but I'm not so much of an ass as to interrupt two dates in one day." He gives me an easy no-hard-feelings grin. "I stole your man away at lunch; I won't do so at dinner as well."

Matt's smile is forced, his hand pressing hard against my back. "Better than you stealing away my woman."

I stiffen, shocked at both Matt's lack of charm in front of an important potential client, as well as my visceral, pleased reaction at being called his woman.

Still, we're here for a reason, and he's *very* close to screwing it all up.

"Matt," I murmur in warning under my breath.

He smiles a bit wider, still focused on the billionaire. "Normally I wouldn't worry, but you're just about the only other man who can afford her."

I can't stop my gasp from slipping out. Nor can I disguise the fact that it's a gasp of pain.

I don't know how it happened, but somehow over the course of the past few days, my shield has been slowing lowering, and now it's gone.

I did what I promised I'd never let him do—hurt me. *Again.*

I swallow and manage to stand, grabbing my purse off the back of the stool, all but shoving away Matt's hand.

"Sabrina—"

I pretend he's not there, my attention focused on Jarod through what I'm horrified to realize is a sheen of tears. "It was nice speaking with you. I appreciate the drinks."

"Of course," he murmurs, his brow furrowing in confusion. "And really, I was just leaving. If you two want to—"

"No, I was just leaving," I say.

And then I do. My chin might be wobbling, but I keep it high as I walk out of the restaurant and onto Pine Street.

Away from Matt Cannon.

17

Matt

Tuesday Evening, September 26

"Sabrina. Shit. Sabrina!"

She's halfway down the block before I can catch up with her, my fingers grabbing hold of her arm and pulling her around.

What I see there rocks me back a step.

Sabrina Cross is *crying*.

She shoves a hand against my shoulder. "*Don't.* Don't talk to me, don't touch me, don't ever call me again."

I run my free hand through my hair, still holding her arm with the other. I'm not letting her get away. Not when she looks like this.

"What did I—"

"He's the only other man who can afford me?" she says, her scathing tone doing nothing to hide her hurt.

"What—"

Oh. Oh fuck.

Fuck fuck fuck.

Of all the boneheaded things I could have said . . .

I lift my hand to her other arm, holding both her shoulders, desperately needing to make her understand. "No," I say firmly. "That's not what I meant."

She pulls away with a harsh laugh. "Whatever. You made it clear four years ago what you thought of me."

I groan. "Not that again—"

"Yes again," she shouts, not caring that a handful of passersby are staring at us wide-eyed. "You may want to forget what you said that morning, but I can't. You said that I must be worth every penny. You said it after we slept together, like I was a common—"

"Don't say it," I growl. "Do not call yourself that."

"Why not?" she challenges. "You practically did."

"You heard what you wanted to hear, then and now," I say, my own voice raising to a shout. "Back then I only meant that you were damn good at your job. You'd told me just hours before that your job was to be anything to anyone, for a price, and that night you were everything to me."

She snorts and opens her mouth to argue, but I talk over her.

"And tonight, I was referring to our shopping expedition. The one where I spent *three thousand dollars* on clothes for you. Wasn't that the point of that whole scheme? So people would think we were a couple? That I doted on you?"

"You've never doted on anyone but yourself your entire life," she says.

Her voice has calmed slightly, and I nearly sag with relief, knowing that while she's still pissed, at least she seems to maybe believe that I wasn't telling Lanham she was a damned paid escort service.

"Maybe not," I grant her. "Doting's not my thing, but neither is hurting people. And I hurt you."

"You didn't—"

"I *did*," I interrupt. "I did and I'm sorry, Sabrina. I just got . . ."

She lifts her eyebrows in question when I don't finish, and I sigh in frustration—at her, at Lanham, at myself.

"I saw you talking to him, and—"

"You were worried I'd blow your cover."

"Hell yes, I was worried!" I explode.

Worried you'd be happy with someone other than me. Worried that I could lose you, even before I really had you.

I shove the thoughts aside, clinging to the safety of anger instead. "The entire reason we have a fucking contract is so that people like Lanham will think we're together, that I've settled down, that I'm not blowing money on lap dances and drugs. Instead, I look over and see my girlfriend flirting with the very client I'm trying to win over."

"Well it's a damn good thing I was," she snaps. "Because after you went all caveman on him, I can't imagine he'll be dying to work with you."

She's right. There's a very real chance I've just blown any possibility at getting Lanham on my roster, and the hell of it is . . .

I can't seem to care.

I can't seem to see anything but her with him, looking for all the world like she was enjoying herself with another man.

"Everything okay here?" Ian's quiet voice comes from behind me.

I let my chin drop to my chest for a moment. I love Ian like a brother. I do. He's my best friend. But sometimes . . . *sometimes* . . .

I envy him. I envy him the role of Sabrina's savior. Her friend.

I envy that he's the one she runs to. That he's the one who gets to look out for her. Protect her.

Meanwhile, *I'm* the one who hurts her. The one she needs protecting *from*.

I turn toward him. His hands are in his pockets, his stance casual, his eyes anything but.

I give him a nod. "Yeah. We're fine."

He studies me for a moment before his gaze flicks to Sabrina.

I hear her swallow. "Yeah, Ian. We're good."

"You sure? Because—"

"Ian." Her voice is firm. "Go back inside. Please."

My head snaps toward her. I'd expected her to take the out he offered, to retreat under his wing where he protects all the childhood secrets the two of them harbor.

I know Ian's. I don't know hers.

I only know that whatever shit the two of them went through together, it bonded them. Until Lara, Sabrina always came first with Ian.

And Ian's always come first with Sabrina.

Until . . . now?

I turn back to see Ian frown in confusion. "But—"

"This is between Matt and me. I'm handling it."

He sighs. "Fine. Don't kill each other."

"No promises," she says with a small smile. "Give Lara my apologies?"

"Sure," he says, smiling back.

His smile disappears when he looks at me. I don't blame him. Sabrina's putting on a good show, but there's a fragility about her right now that I've never seen before. From the worried look on his face, I don't think he has, either.

We both wait until Ian's moved out of earshot before continuing our conversation.

I turn back to her. "Sabrina, can we please—"

"How much longer?"

"What?" I ask, not following.

"Our contract. Me pretending to be in love with you." Her voice is tired. "The contract says until the gala. Is that still the case? Because if not, I'd be happy to give you a prorated rate."

I feel the sudden urge to punch the brick wall beside me. I'm trying to talk to the damn woman, and all she cares about are contracts and prorated costs.

"Yes," I snap. "I need you until the gala."

I don't know if it's true. I don't even know what I need or want anymore, but I know letting her out of this contract now, when things are like this between us, would be a mistake.

"Fine," she says coolly, taking a step back. "You'll let me know when my next scheduled appearance is?"

"Sabrina. Come on."

She moves toward the curb and lifts her hand to hail an approaching cab. "I'd appreciate it if you stick with the twenty-four-hours' notice going forward. I think today proved that last-minute arrangements are hardly working in your favor."

The cab stops, and out of habit, I go to open the door for her, but she beats me to it. "Seventy-second and Park, please," she tells the driver.

"Sabrina, I really am sorr—"

She shuts the door on the rest of my apology.

Frustrated as hell, I watch the taillights of her cab until they disappear from sight, taking her back to her apartment uptown.

And even then, I stay still a bit longer, replaying Kennedy's words from earlier over in my head.

Everything you've ever wanted . . .

I'm not sure about that.

I'm not sure about that at all.

18

Sabrina

Thursday Evening, September 28

My iPhone continues its relentless buzz from the counter, and Juno gives the phone a baleful look before giving me one that's a bit . . . scolding.

I scrape my hair into a messy bun atop my head as I give the dog a look right back. "I'm not answering it."

Juno sits. *At least put the phone on "Do Not Disturb."*

I shake my head. "I fed the beast. I have to live with the consequences. It'll remind me to be smarter next year."

Juno slumps to the floor with a sigh, resting her snout on her paw as she avoids eye contact.

She's disappointed in me, and that's just fine. I'm disappointed in me, too.

Honestly, will I never learn?

Today is my mother's birthday. Yeah. As in the mother who I have almost nothing to do with. The one who was a mother by biological contribution only.

Every year as September 28 approaches, I tell myself that *this* year I'll let the day come and go without doing a damn thing.

But some stupid part of me, the part that's still nine and hoping the homemade birdhouse or carefully constructed bead necklace will win her over, sends a gift.

I've moved beyond the homemade stuff. She's not worth the effort. I know that much, at least. And while the online shopping process is infinitely easier . . . it has created a whole other monster.

It never fails. The first text message or voice mail is a thank-you (mind you, it's the only time I hear from her all year).

The second message comes an hour later and is the guilt trip: You know, the more I think about it, the purse is just too extravagant. I appreciate the offer, but if it's all the same to you, I'll think I'll sell it. I could use the cash for more practical things.

Now, don't applaud her just yet. The tone shifts in the third message: Call me back already. Things have been tough around here lately, and I could use some help.

The fourth message is where things get really nasty: I don't know how I raised someone so selfish. You can afford a fancy leather purse, but you can't be bothered to make sure I have basic necessities?

Now, let's get a few things straight. First, she didn't raise anyone. I raised myself.

Second, she has basic necessities. How do I know? Because I paid off her mortgage. I pay for a twice-weekly grocery service that delivers everything she needs to make easy, healthy meals for herself.

That's right, I put a roof over her head and food on the table.

The first one is repayment for the little that she did do for me and my half brothers back in the day. The second is a bonus.

The messages will escalate for the next twenty-four hours, shifting from promises to pay me back for whatever "loan" she wants (fact: she won't), to angry rants, to sobbing guilt trips.

Also, if you're wondering, she never actually sells the jewelry or handbags I send her. We're friends on Facebook, and she's addicted to the platform, posting a dozen pictures a day. Most of them feature the Coach purse, the earrings from Bergdorf, the Swarovski watch.

Why do I do it?

Good freaking question.

As far as why I don't just turn off my damn phone? It's like I told the dog . . . I keep hoping that I'll teach myself a lesson.

She may not ever change, but I can.

"What are we eating?" I ask Juno, opening the fridge.

Her head pops up, tail wagging enthusiastically at the prospect of getting something other than kibble tonight.

"Hmm." I purse my lips and survey the meager supplies. "How do we feel about takeout?"

Juno's tail wags faster.

I start to go for my phone to order something from my delivery app when someone knocks on my door.

My heart leaps. The last time someone knocked on my door out of the blue, I ended up agreeing to play fake girlfriend for my mortal enemy. A decision that's had some extremely painful consequences.

Of course, it may not be Matt.

Hell. It's definitely Matt. I *feel* it, and that's annoying. I've been anticipating it, and that's even more annoying.

Juno, for her part, is losing her mind, alternating between frantic barks and throwing herself at the door.

I do the requisite safety check through the peephole, my stomach doing a full-on flip when I see Matt is indeed standing there.

With flowers.

I open the door, not even remotely regretting the way Matt's required to take a step back from the force of my dog colliding with his legs.

"Juno, darling," Matt says, lowering to give the dog attention. "I brought you something."

Leaning against the doorjamb, I watch as he pulls a dog biscuit from his pocket. Juno munches it enthusiastically, nuzzling Matt's chest as she chews.

Matt laughs at the crumbs spraying everywhere, oblivious and uncaring that his cashmere sweater is now covered in slobber, cookie crumbs, and dog fur.

I know the sweater's cashmere, because I was with him when he bought it. I was right. It does match his eyes. Eyes that slowly lift from the dog until they find mine.

"Hi," he says.

"Hi." I nod at the flowers. "What's the story there?"

He stands and looks down at the pink roses. There are at least two dozen flawless buds. "I brought them for your doorman downstairs. Juan? Turns out he prefers tulips. Seemed a shame to waste them, so . . ." He flicks his wrist toward me, extending them.

Unable to resist, I reach for them, nodding for him to come in. He does, Juno unabashedly sniffing at his pocket for more cookies.

"Sorry, love," Matt says, giving the dog a pat on the head. "Just the one."

Juno huffs and trots to her food bowl, resigned to the fact that there are no more treats to be had and the takeout's been delayed.

I go into the kitchen and pull a vase from the cupboard. Matt follows. "What are your favorite flowers, anyway? Ian didn't know."

"Pretty ones," I say, setting the vase in the sink and turning on the water. "Flowers are always nice to receive, no matter the kind."

"You were supposed to say pink roses and be very impressed that I got it right on the first try."

Since my back is to him, I allow a small smile as I pull scissors out of a drawer to trim the stems.

It's been two days since our fight on the sidewalk after the Jarod Lanham run-in, and I've been avoiding him. At first, it was because I was still mad and hurting. After that, I avoided him because . . .

I take a deep breath and turn around. "I have something to say to you."

His gaze drops to my hand. "Any chance you can say it *after* you've put down the scissors?"

"I'm sorry," I say in a rush, ignoring his attempts to lighten the mood. "I jumped to conclusions based on our history, and I acted horribly unprofessional. You hired me to convince people that we were in a relationship, and I jeopardized that."

Matt smiles. "Cross, I'm pretty sure anyone witnessing that fight was even *more* convinced we're in a relationship."

I turn around and begin to cut open the cellophane containing the bouquet. "I thought of that. I even mentally added 'lovers' spat' to my list of strategies on making a relationship seem more authentic. Still, I—"

Matt moves behind me, and though he doesn't touch me, I can feel his closeness. "I don't care that you acted unprofessionally. I care that I hurt you."

"I was mad. That's all," I say, trimming the ends of the roses into the sink.

"That's crap," he says softly.

It is crap. But the last thing I want to do is revisit the pain that ripped through me that night. Or the fact that this man is the only person to ever elicit that kind of hurt.

I certainly don't want to explore why that's so.

"Is that what the flowers are for?" I ask, beginning to place the stems in the vase. "Apology flowers?"

"The first dozen are 'I'm sorry' flowers, yeah."

I give him a look over my shoulder. "And the second?"

He comes around to my side, the heels of his hands braced on my kitchen counter as he watches me arrange the roses. "'Favor' flowers," he says finally.

"Ah," I say, stepping back and tilting my head to make sure my arrangement is even, before taking it to my kitchen table. "'Favor' flowers, also known as 'buttering up' flowers. Generally preceding a highly unpleasant request."

"You have no idea," he grumbles, running a hand through his hair.

There's something in his tone, a touch of vulnerability I'm not used to hearing from a man who usually has boundless energy and charm.

"What's up?" I ask, sensing I need to be just a little bit careful with him.

He sucks in his cheeks for a moment, thinking. "Got anything to drink?"

"Of course." I motion to the bar cart. "Or I have white wine in the fridge, red on the rack."

He goes to the bar cart, selecting a bottle of Grey Goose. "You don't keep this in the freezer?"

"I like the vodka to melt the ice just a little. I think the martini tastes better slightly diluted."

He's distracted, barely seems to hear me. "You want one?"

"No, thanks. I've got an open bottle of white in the fridge."

He pours me a glass of wine first before going about the process of making himself a drink. Strange, how normal the sight of Matt Cannon fixing a martini in my apartment is starting to feel.

I wait until he's dropped his lemon twist in the cocktail glass before nudging him again. "So . . . the favor?"

"Right."

He takes a sip of the drink, his attention shifting to my phone, which is starting to buzz on the counter right next to him.

He glances at it when I don't make a move to pick it up. "A Rochelle is calling. Are we answering?"

"We're ignoring."

He raises his eyebrows. "Are we talking about it?"

"We are not."

He gives a faint smile, but I get the feeling my answer disappoints him. As though he was hoping I'd share more details.

I want to tell him that my hesitancy isn't about him—that I don't talk about my mother with anyone—but that'll only derail the conversation from whatever it is he's reluctant to talk about.

I wait.

"So, I'm hoping I can talk you into coming to a dinner with me on Saturday."

"Um, sure?" I say, taking a drink of my wine. "That's the deal, right? Up until the gala, I show up wherever you need me. And you're well within the twenty-four-hour advance-notice requirement." I smile. "You could have saved yourself the second dozen flowers."

He doesn't smile back. "You haven't heard all of it yet."

"Cannon, I once took tango classes with a known mobster as a favor to the NYPD. I think I can handle whatever you throw at me."

"The dinner on Saturday is with my parents. At their house in Connecticut."

"Whoa." I take a large swallow of wine.

"Yeah," he says in a tired tone. "You know your girl Georgie, the one who put our 'relationship' on the gossip circuit? My mother is on that circuit. There's not a single item of Manhattan gossip she isn't privy to, and she's insisted I bring my 'girlfriend' to dinner."

"Meting the parents is one tall order. But if it'll help sell the story—"

"That's the thing," he interrupts. "My dad use to be plugged into the Wall Street scene, and by extension, so was my mother. But he retired last year, and mostly they're wrapped up in their Connecticut social scene with other retirees. Golf, book clubs, that sort of thing."

"So, us having dinner with them won't do anything to help salvage your professional reputation?"

He lifts a shoulder. "I mean, in theory, my dad could mention it to someone important during his daily round of golf, but . . . no, not really."

"So why not just tell them the truth?"

He winces. "They're not really those kind of parents. Also, full disclosure, my motives are . . . selfish. After years of trying to be younger than she is, my mom's realized she's the only one of her friends without grandbaby pictures to show off."

"Oh no."

He nods. "Yeah. She's been trying to set me up with every single woman in the Northeast, from her hairdresser to the remaining single daughters of their friends."

"Having a girlfriend gets her off your back," I conclude.

"Bingo."

I blow out a long breath as I consider this. I should be freaking out by the very suggestion, but instead I find myself intrigued. The chance to find out more about where Matt came from, what shaped him . . . it's appealing.

"No hard feelings if you say no," Matt says. "I know I don't have the right to ask you as a . . . friend."

The way he hesitates over the last word does something funny to my stomach, as though he wants to be friends but isn't sure it's possible.

It's possible.

"You know, for future reference, you really should have brought two dozen 'favor' flowers for this kind of ask. And maybe jewelry."

A slow grin starts to spread over his face. "You'll do it?"

"Yes. If nothing else, to save all those other women from the agony of being fixed up with you."

And to save myself the agony of knowing you're dating someone else.

"Thank you," he says in relief. "Seriously, thank you. And I'd love to tell you you won't regret it, but in the interest of honesty, you totally will."

I laugh. "Candor appreciated."

He takes another sip of his drink. "Well, I'll get out of your hair. Let you get back to your evening."

I nod, but instead of feeling relieved that he's leaving, I feel a little melancholy at the thought of it.

"You can finish your drink," I say, just as my phone starts to buzz again.

I walk to the counter and pick it up, turn it to "Do Not Disturb," then set the phone aside.

For a long minute, we say nothing. Finally, I look up at him. "Rochelle is my mother."

He studies my expression, then nods. "Okay."

I take a deep breath. "And I don't want to talk about her."

"Okay," he says without hesitation.

It's the perfect response.

"Cannon?"

"Yup."

I look down at my wine. "Juno and I were going to order takeout. I was thinking Chinese."

"Okay?" This time it's a question.

"You can stay. Eat with us. I mean, if you want." I look up.

"Okay." This time it's not a question. And it's paired with a happy grin that makes my heart feel like flying.

19

Matt

Saturday Evening, September 30

You know how snobby people talk about the distinction between old money and new money, as though it's a thing?

It's definitely a thing.

I know, because I grew up surrounded by the latter.

Neither of my parents grew up rich. My mom's solidly middle class from Boise. My dad's the son of two schoolteachers in Oklahoma.

They met in New York when my mom was a flight attendant on a stopover and my dad was staying at the same hotel, celebrating getting his first job offer from an investment firm. (My knack for numbers comes straight from the old man.)

A one-night stand turned into a long-distance relationship, which turned into an engagement, which turned into the fanciest wedding Boise had ever seen, courtesy of my dad moving quickly up the Wall Street food chain.

They'd moved to New York, done the requisite big-city couple thing for a few years as my dad got more firmly established in the financial scene. My dad doesn't talk much about those days, but my mom claims they were wildly in love, the kind of all-consuming love that makes you blind to reality.

Eventually, Mom's biological clock started ticking (her words not mine, because I'd prefer never to think of it), and they'd moved to a Connecticut McMansion, i.e. a cookie-cutter, pristine new-construction house that looked almost identical to all their neighbors'.

I'd been born shortly after. Shortly after *that*, they moved to another McMansion, this one slightly larger. I'd spent most of my youth there, and when I left for college, they moved to yet another house, this one in a gated community and bigger than the other two combined, never mind that it was just the two of them.

And here's where the "new money" cliché comes into play: my parents spend money just to spend it. Or maybe to let other people know they have it? I've never really been able to figure it out. They've never kept a car longer than a year. It always has to be the newest model. My mom gets a new Dior purse every season, plus a matching wallet. My dad doesn't just have a Rolex, he collects them. And talks about them.

You think I'm being hard on them? Perhaps. After all, I never wanted for anything. My first car was a brand-new red BMW convertible. For my eighteenth birthday party, my parents flew twelve of my friends and me to Aspen for a ski trip.

The money doesn't bother me. Neither does the way they spend it, not really. It's the fact that somewhere along the line, they let money replace morals. And integrity.

Don't believe me? Just wait and see.

"You might have mentioned that you weren't going to say a single word on the drive up," Sabrina says, breaking the silence in the car.

I glance over at the passenger side, not at all sure how I feel about her presence. On the one hand, I'm relieved for the company. On the other hand, I don't know that I'm ready for anyone to see this part of my life. I've kept it private for so long.

"Sorry," I say, drumming my thumbs on the steering wheel. "Spending time with both my parents together always makes me tense."

"You don't mention them much."

"Probably for the same reason you don't mention yours."

She snorts and turns her head to look out the window. "I doubt it."

I don't push her. Someday, she'll tell me all about Rochelle and the shadows in her eyes whenever someone mentions her childhood, but now is not the time.

"You look nice," I say, turning down the radio as I take the exit ramp off the freeway.

"He says, an hour and a half after picking me up," she teases.

"I was too busy trying to figure out if that dress is one I bought for you."

She smiles enigmatically. "It might be."

We stop at a red light, and I turn to her more fully, my gaze appreciating the way the slim-fitting dark-purple dress hugs her curves. "You think of me when you put it on?"

Her eyes narrow slightly, as though sensing the question I really want to ask: *Will you think of me when you take it off?*

Or better yet, *Can* I *take it off?*

She tilts her head to the stoplight. "Light's green, Lothario."

Her voice is a little bit huskier than before, and I grin, betting I'm not the only one who's been suffering from her no-hookups rule.

There's no time to dwell—or fantasize—about that, though. A couple of minutes later, I roll down the window and enter the key code that opens the gate to my parents' cul-de-sac.

Sabrina whistles as we pass the first enormous house. "Very Stepford."

"Yeah, well, there's a reason that's set that in Connecticut," I grumble, lifting a hand in greeting toward one of my parents' neighbors, who gives us a wave that's both friendly and nosy as hell.

"Is it really?" she asks, looking over at me.

"Yup."

"Huh," she says thoughtfully. "I have to say, I sort of thought this lifestyle only existed in movies."

I pull into my parents' driveway. "In a few minutes, you're going to wish it did."

She laughs lightly. "It can't be that bad."

I nod at the Lexus that's pulled into the driveway just ahead of us as a woman steps out of the driver's side. "See her?"

"Yeah. That your mom?" Sabrina asks, her hand lifting to smooth her hair.

I'd grin at the atypically nervous gesture if my stomach wasn't so knotted in dread. Sabrina's about to see what my story's really about, and it isn't pretty.

"That's my dad's former assistant."

"Oh." Sabrina's hand drops, and she undoes her seat belt. "She looks nice."

I lift my hand to wave at the woman in tight jeans and a low-cut white sweater. "She's also my father's mistress."

"What?" Sabrina's head whips toward me, but I'm already pushing open the car door and stepping out.

"Matt, sweetie. It's been too long." She grins and beckons me forward, arms spread for a hug.

"Felicia, good to see you," I say, kissing her cheek and embracing her.

Felicia's hands find my shoulders, and she pulls back to study me. Then she smiles wider. "You look happy. Well, your shoulders are a bit tense, but your eyes are happy."

Felicia's gaze shifts to Sabrina, who's stepped out of the car, looking composed instead of shell-shocked, God bless her.

"And this must be Sabrina. I've heard so much about you."

I introduce the two women. "Felicia Levin, this is my girlfriend, Sabrina Cross."

Sabrina extends a hand, but Felicia ignores it and goes in for a hug. "I'm so glad Matt's found someone to help him settle down. We were all so tired of him moving from woman to woman with less care than he did swapping out his cuff links."

It's a bold accusation from someone who's been having an affair with a married man for a couple dozen years, but Sabrina's smile never wavers.

A tinny version of Beyoncé's "Halo" interrupts the moment, and Felicia looks toward her still-open car door. "Oh, that's my daughter calling. She's getting married next month, and she's a basket case. You guys go on inside, tell your parents I'll be along shortly." She trots back to her car in her platform sandals and leans in to grab her cell phone. "Bridget, honey. I've told you, we can always let the dress out a bit if we need to . . . No, you are not fat . . ."

I set an arm to Sabrina's back, propelling her toward my parents' front door. The sooner we get this started, the sooner we can leave.

"Does your mom know?"

"Yup."

"Does she care?"

"If she does, she'd be a hypocrite. She carried on with my Little League coach for years before switching to my history tutor. Then it was one of my dad's golf buddies, and I'm pretty sure there was a pool boy in there somewhere."

Sabrina looks up at me as I ring the doorbell, and I stand very still, very tense, bracing for the questions, the judgment, the horror at the salacious shallowness I grew up in.

"Cannon."

I don't look at her. I can't. "Yeah?"

She leans toward me slightly and whispers, "You had a history tutor?"

I let out a startled laugh. Her response is so unexpected and so fucking perfect that I do the only thing I can do.

I bend my head to hers and kiss her.

20

Sabrina

Saturday Evening, September 30

Matt's mouth is warm and firm on mine, and any thought I have to remind him we're no longer hooking up goes out the window when his hand gently cups the back of my head, pulling me closer.

His lips nudge mine apart, and mine respond, welcoming his kiss as though I'm made for it. Made for kissing him.

Matt's tongue touches mine, and a little moan slips out . . .

Just as the front door opens.

"Oh! Oh my!"

I push away from Matt, baffled by the heat flooding my cheeks. Oh, this is what blushing feels like. I haven't felt it in . . . forever.

I turn to find a thin blonde woman grinning at me. "Matthew Cannon, I haven't seen you embarrass a girl like this since you took Brianne Ross to prom and whispered something in her ear that made her blush redder than tomato sauce."

I turn to Matt. "What'd you whisper?"

Matt's mother lets out a delighted laugh. "Oh, I can see why he likes you. You're Sabrina, obviously. And I'm Maureen Cannon, Matt's mother, obviously."

Actually, there's really nothing obvious about it, considering I met a woman in the driveway who acted just as motherly toward Matt. But I don't say this. *Obviously.*

"Mother," Matt says, bending to kiss his mom's cheek as he steps inside. "Good to see you."

She wraps her arms around him and gives a quick squeeze. "I'm so glad you're here. Okay, Sabrina, come in, come in. Get your coat off, and let's get you a drink."

"Felicia's here," Matt says, helping me out of my trench coat. "Bridget called, so she'll be in in a minute."

"Oh, poor Bridget," Maureen says with a regretful sigh as she reaches out to take my coat from Matt. She looks at me. "Poor thing's put on a good amount of weight just before the wedding."

"Mom." Matt's voice is gently chiding.

"I don't say it to be mean!" Maureen insists. "She can't help she has her mother's body type."

It's a catty little jab, to be sure, but there doesn't seem to be much malice behind it. Instead it's like the way I've heard competitive sisters talk about one another—little put-downs here and there to lift their own egos but no real venom. Almost as though she's simply resigned to the other woman's presence at family dinners.

Maureen turns her head slightly toward a hallway on her right. "Gary! Your son's here!"

A masculine voice replies immediately. "Matt! Get in here a sec—I want to show you something."

Matt gives me an apologetic look. "He has a new laptop. Ten bucks says he doesn't want to show me anything, just ask me how to use it, all while pretending he's teaching me."

I smile to reassure him I'll be fine with his mother. "Hopefully you're better with computers than history."

Maureen lets out a laugh as Matt makes a *ha-ha* face and heads down the hall to wherever his father is.

"Told you about that, did he?" Maureen says as she motions for me to follow her. "I'd forgotten all about that. It was the funniest thing seeing his face when he realized he'd gotten a C in British history. I thought he was going to pass out."

"His first C?"

She rolls her eyes. "First anything that wasn't an A plus. Though he always had to work a bit harder on anything that wasn't numbers. He's like his dad that way. Calculator for a brain, but when it comes to reading and writing, he's merely average."

"Heard that!" Matt calls from somewhere.

"Sit, sit," his mom says, ignoring her son as she leads me into a fussily decorated living room. "What can I get you to drink? Wine, cocktail, soda?"

"White wine would be great," I say, setting my purse on a bench by the door. "You have a beautiful home."

I say it to be polite more than anything. It's not that the Cannon home isn't beautiful, it's just . . . intense.

The floor in the entryway is white marble, the chandelier the size of a small car. And maybe I've just grown used to the minimalist decor of most New York apartments, but there seems to be stuff *everywhere*. Pretty stuff—gorgeous centerpieces, tall vases, fresh flowers, ornate boxes, gold-framed art on the walls.

But still . . . stuff.

I wouldn't go so far as to call the home stifling, but I can't imagine living here. Hell, for that matter, I can't imagine Matt living here. I haven't put much thought into Matt's background before, but I definitely wouldn't have pictured this. Not the lavishness, and certainly not the apparently open nature of his parents' marriage.

It provides a little glimpse into the man that I haven't seen before, and I'm not at all sure what to do with the new information. I know only that the tense man who picked me up this evening is nothing like the devil-may-care charmer I've known for years. I can't help but wonder which is the real Matt.

I wonder if he even knows.

It's hard to believe the guy's turned out as normal as he has, though I suppose his parents' choices did leave a lasting mark: his wariness of all things relationships and marriage.

"So, I hear from Matt you guys met through a mutual friend," Maureen says, coming back with a glass of white wine for each of us and patting the seat next to her on a white-and-gold love seat.

I sit beside her and cross my legs. "Yes. I grew up with one of his coworkers."

"Ian, right?"

I nod.

"He's a handsome one. Well, so is that Kennedy, though his parents are somewhat standoffish. Especially his mother. Did you know, we were at the same fund-raiser as they were a couple years ago, and I thought it would be nice if we got to know each other. But let me tell you, that woman . . ."

I tune her out as she prattles on about the evils of Kennedy's mother, interjecting only the occasional nod and "mm-hmm."

It's not that Maureen Cannon is a bad woman. She's friendly and seems to truly adore her son. But she's also self-absorbed, a bit gossipy, and, even though it's none of my business, I just can't fully embrace a woman who cheats on her husband.

Even if he cheats on her as well.

Poor Matt. I wonder how long he's known. He mentioned his mom sleeping with his Little League coach, and I can only hope he learned about it long after the fact. It'd be a hell of a thing for a kid to grow up with.

My mother slept around plenty as well, but at least she had the good sense never to get married.

"I'm sorry, I just hijacked our entire conversation," Maureen says, touching my arm. "Tell me about you. I confess I looked you up, but I didn't learn much about your people."

My people?

My tolerance for Maureen Cannon dips a tiny bit lower. I suppose on some level, I should be relieved that she's bought the facade I've built for myself. That she sees me as one of them.

I'm not surprised. I've made darn sure people see exactly what I want them to see: a polished, poised, successful woman who wears the right clothes, knows the right people, makes the right small talk.

Still, tonight, the whole thing feels vaguely distasteful. Perhaps because I'm fairly certain she wouldn't be nearly as welcoming if she knew my real background.

"I'm from Philadelphia." I take a sip of my wine.

"Oh, Philly!" she says with fake delight. "Do you go back often?"

"No."

"So your family . . . Are they no longer—"

"Mom."

I look up in relief as Matt steps into the room, along with Felicia and an older man who's obviously his father.

If Matt got his mom's eyes, he got his dad's everything else. Gary Cannon is the spitting image of what I imagine Matt'll look like in thirty or so years.

I stand to greet him, and he gives me a firm handshake. "Welcome."

"Thanks for having me, Mr. Cannon."

"Gary, please." He says it with a smile, but my first impression is that he has all of Matt's looks but none of his son's charms. There's a wooden, tired quality about him.

Who knows, perhaps it's decades' worth of stress from sleeping with one woman while being married to another?

Matt pours himself a drink from the sideboard as Felicia and Maureen make small talk about Felicia's daughter's wedding. The conversation is so sugary sweet my teeth ache.

Matt catches my gaze and rolls his eyes. I give him a quick smile in return. Weird and unexpected as the whole situation is, there's something oddly nice about being Matt's partner in all of this.

Not to mention it's surprisingly comforting to realize I'm not the only one with a background that isn't *Leave It to Beaver* perfect.

"Maureen," Gary says, interrupting his wife's assessment of the perils of Felicia's daughter not offering a gluten-free meal option at the wedding. "When are we eating?"

Maureen doesn't miss a beat at her husband's rudeness, but her smile is as wide as it is brittle. "They've only just gotten here, Gary. I'm sure they didn't drive an hour and a half to be rushed out of here."

Matt's expression indicates he'd like nothing better, but he says nothing as he sips his drink.

"I thought we'd have hors d'oeuvres on the patio. The fire pit's going, and we just had those new heaters installed. I've got a nice baked brie—"

"That's fine," Gary interrupts, heading toward the door.

Felicia follows him, patting Matt's arm affectionately, almost motherly, as she does so.

I glance at Maureen to see if she minds her husband's mistress acting like a second mother to her only son, but she merely smiles at me. "More wine, dear?"

"Yes," Matt answers for me. "The whole bottle might be good."

Maureen lets out a clueless laugh as she heads back into the kitchen.

Matt comes toward me, his face unreadable. "You okay?"

"I'm not going to say this won't go down as one of the weirdest evenings I've ever experienced, but it's solid entertainment."

I'm relieved when he smiles. "I should have told you everything. But I was afraid you wouldn't come."

"A safe bet," I say as we follow his dad and Felicia toward the back of the house. "But for future reference, when it's a real girlfriend who might not be quite so understanding . . ."

"I know, I know. Skip the flowers and go for jewelry."

"Actually . . ." I lift up and kiss his cheek. "I liked the flowers. A lot."

I step out onto the patio to hide my embarrassment at my spontaneity. What is with me? I'm acting far too much like an actual besotted girlfriend than a pretend one. It's very . . . confusing.

The heaters Maureen mentioned wonderfully heat the Cannons' outdoor seating area against the late-September chill. I join Matt's family by the fire pit, both pleased and alarmed when he sits beside me, close enough for our knees to touch.

Pleased, because I like the intimacy of the moment.

Alarmed . . . because I also like *him*.

21

Matt

Saturday Night, September 30

Sabrina and I haven't spoken much on the drive back, but it's a companionable sort of silence.

By the time we get back to the city, it's nearly eleven, and the crisp dryness of the early evening has given way to a relentless rain that soothes away the sharp edges of the night.

Then again, that could be the effect of the woman beside me. I'd never have thought that Sabrina Cross could have a calming quality. From the very beginning, she's always been the fuel that lights my flame, the spark that sets me on fire.

Sabrina sighs as I turn onto Park toward her apartment building. "I use to love the rain."

I glance over, the city lights playing shadows off her profile. "Use to?"

"Until I got a dog."

"Juno's not a fan?"

"She's fine with rain as long as there's no thunder. *And* if there's no umbrella within twenty feet of her. Oh, and did I mention she freaks out if I wear a hood?" She touches her hair. "Bye-bye, good hair day."

"I'll take her."

She looks over. "What?"

"I'll walk Juno."

"You are not walking my dog."

"Why not? I've done it before when you were out of town."

"Yes, but I didn't ask you to. I asked Kate. She betrayed me."

"Yeah, a real Judas, that one. Look, you didn't ask me then, and you're not asking me now. I'm volunteering."

"You have your car."

"Which—and brace yourself for this news flash—*can be parked*."

"There's not that much street parking. My apartment building has a garage, but it's . . . expensive," she finishes as I pull into said garage.

"Really?" I say, rolling down the window and punching the button for a ticket. "You have no qualms about my dropping four digits on your clothing, but you're worried about—" I glance at the sign with the parking prices. "Damn, that *is* expensive parking."

"Right?" She unbuckles her seat belt. "If you turn around now, you can sweet-talk the attendant, tell her that you came in here by accident."

I ignore her as I pull into an available spot and turn off the engine. She huffs. I grin.

"Okay, fine. But you taking my dog out does not make us even," she says as we climb out of the car and walk toward the elevators. "That dinner was horrendous."

I laugh. "It really was, wasn't it?"

"Does Felicia always show up for dinner?"

"No, but it's become more frequent the past couple years."

"Has your mom ever brought one of her . . . guys?"

"Nope. Felicia's divorced, but my mom's guys have always been married. I don't think their wives would be keen on them coming over for a cozy dinner party."

She shakes her head as we step into the elevator. "You know, I've seen a lot of weird stuff in Manhattan. Open marriages aren't nearly as uncommon as you'd think. But this is the first time I've seen the other woman join the family for dinner, complete with son and new girlfriend."

"You're welcome for the novel experience." I keep my voice light, but I feel her watching me.

"Does it bother you?"

I look toward her without moving my head. "Would you believe me if I said I'm used to it?"

She considers this for a moment. "Yes. But that's not what I asked."

We step onto her floor, but it's not until she digs her keys out of her purse that I answer the question. "Yeah. Yeah, it bothers me."

She nods in understanding, and I'm relieved that she doesn't press me to say more.

Instead, we let ourselves be greeted by an ecstatic Juno, who's so busy bounding in circles that I can barely get her leash on.

"You're sure you don't mind?" Sabrina says as the dog tugs me toward the door.

"You endured my mother's dry lamb chops and my dad's mistress singing an ABBA medley. I've got this. Keys?" She tosses them to me, and I catch them in midair.

Juno charges full speed through the hall, paces impatiently in the elevator, and then shoots across the lobby. Once outside, she slows her roll. She may not hate the rain, but she definitely doesn't love it. She does her business quickly and efficiently before dragging me back toward the door.

Even still, we're sopping wet by the time we get back inside. Juan's working again tonight, and he lifts an idle hand in greeting as I pass. I grin, wondering how Sabrina would feel about the fact that her doorman is officially and thoroughly used to me.

Even if I didn't already know where Sabrina lived, Juno knows the way. I let her drag me to the apartment, where her tail wags impatiently for me to dig the key out of my pocket.

I let us both inside and unclip the dog's leash.

When I straighten, my eyes find Sabrina in the kitchen, and my heart stops with a pang of longing. She's already changed out of her dress and into tight black pants and an oversize sweater, the sleeves pushed up to her elbows. Ugly green socks are on her feet, her hair's pulled back from her face in a messy bun, and she looks . . . beautiful.

I've seen her out of her work clothes before, seen her hair in the same messy knot, but only when I've surprised her by showing up unannounced. Tonight, she knew I'd see her like this when I brought the dog back up.

I suppose it could be a warning sign that she lets me see her in an outfit so obviously nonseductive, but if that's her plan, it's backfiring. Nothing could be more seductive than the realization that she's willing to let her guard down around me.

Finally.

She glances up, a faint smile on her makeup-free lips. "I'm making tea. You want a cup?"

I hate tea, but I feel myself nod.

She looks at me more closely. "You're soaking wet."

I glance down. "Yeah. I'd ask if you have any extra men's clothes stashed around, but I'm not entirely sure I want to know the answer."

"Yes, because I'm sure you've been celibate since we first met," she says, dropping a couple of tea bags into a pot. "I'll get you a towel."

It's more my sweater that's wet than anything, so I pull it off and set it over the back of a chair. I'm standing in just my undershirt as she reenters the living room, tossing a towel at me.

"Thanks." I run the towel over my wet hair. "Where's Juno?"

"Post-poo-in-the-rain routine usually involves rolling on her back on my bedroom rug for a solid five minutes. I've learned not to question it."

Sabrina uses her phone to turn on music, and the soft sounds of a female jazz vocalist I'm not familiar with fill the room. She grabs two mugs and carries them and the teapot into the living room.

Setting them on the ottoman that doubles as her coffee table, she stares at the teapot for a long moment before looking up at me, her expression thoughtful. "Can I ask you something?"

I sit beside her on the couch, careful to keep my distance, terrified of ruining the fragile truce between us. "Sure."

She turns her attention back to the teapot and pours the tea. "Are your parents why you're dead set against marriage?" She smiles faintly and hands me a mug.

I nod in thanks before answering her question. "Probably."

"Probably it's because of your parents?"

I nod. "I mean, it's not quite as simple as my seeing how fucked up their marriage was and making a vow never to follow in their footsteps. But over time, being a part of that—and I was a part of it, not that they ever bothered to notice—it wears on a kid. Hell, it wears on an adult."

I'm braced for the usual lecture—that my parents' mistakes don't have to be my own, that I can't live my life in reaction to someone else's missteps, etc. etc. Everything that every woman or girlfriend has tried to tell me over the years until I finally gave up altogether and made it clear that I didn't want a relationship, period.

But Sabrina doesn't give me any of that. She simply nods. "I get it. As much as I'm rooting for Lara and Ian and wish them the best, the truth is I've seen a hell of a lot more messed-up relationships than I have good ones."

I take a sip of tea. I still hate it, but the warmth is nice, I guess.

She gives a rueful smile at my silence. "Too cynical?"

"No," I say slowly. "I don't disagree. It's just odd to hear it out loud, from someone else. Especially someone who's not as anti-marriage as I am."

"I'm in favor of a certain type of marriage," she clarifies. "The quiet, no-drama kind that doesn't lead to messiness."

"What about sex?"

She looks up sharply. "What about it?"

"This arrangement with your future husband. Does it involve sex?"

"I'd hope so."

I run my tongue over the front of my teeth, surprised at just how much the prospect of her marrying and sleeping with someone else bothers me. I shake my head. "Sex and living together. Sounds a lot like a real marriage to me."

"It is," she says matter-of-factly. "Just without the power to hurt each other."

"But wouldn't it get complicated if you throw sex into the mix? Emotionally, I mean."

"*We* did it," she says, cutting me with a direct look.

"Did we?" I sit back. "Seems to me there was plenty of emotion there, just not a gentle one."

She turns her head toward me. "Hate?"

"Not hate. Never hate. At least not on my part." I smile, letting my gaze drift over her features. She looks younger without her makeup. Softer.

"Anger, though," she says.

"Sure. Some of that. A lot of it, maybe," I agree.

"You ever wonder why? What we were mad at?"

"I've always had a pretty good idea. We hooked up the first night we met, I said something stupid the next morning, you got pissed—rightfully so," I rush to add when she looks ready to interrupt. "And after that . . ." I trail off and take a sip of tea, which, for the record, tastes like dirty water.

"We couldn't quite figure out how to get along," she finishes for me.

"You're one hell of a complicated woman."

"And yet you didn't leave."

"What do you mean?"

She leans forward and stares down at the mug she has yet to sip from. "I've said so many awful things to you, and you to me, and yet you watch my dog when I'm gone. I agree to help you get your life back on track. We look out for each other, even when we're trying desperately to avoid each other."

"Don't forget about the *excellent* sex."

She smiles, and it looks almost shy. "Yeah. Excellent sex."

I reach out and take the mug from her hands, setting it on the ottoman, setting my own beside it. "We going to talk about the fact that I kissed you tonight?"

"I've decided to overlook the breach of contract. You've got one hell of a home life there, Cannon."

"I do. But what's your excuse?"

"For what?"

"For kissing me back."

She gives me an annoyed look. "We're not talking about that."

"Good," I say simply. "Because talking's not at all what I had in mind."

Then I reach out and haul her to me.

22

Sabrina

Saturday Night, September 30

I know.

I know.

We're not supposed to be doing this anymore.

What's more, this was *my* rule. My decision that if we agreed to play pretend relationship, we'd cut our enemies-with-benefits out of the equation.

A rule I decided to break the second he reached for me.

For that matter, I think I decided to break it the moment I asked him to stay for a cup of tea instead of sending him right back out into the rain.

My brain's screaming, *Fool.* My heart's screaming, *Mayday*.

But my body . . . . it knows what it wants—what it *needs*—and it has always needed him.

I've tried to find the same elusive pleasure with someone else, but nobody makes me feel as cherished as he does. Even through the anger, the frustration—or maybe because of those feelings—Matt Cannon's hands on me deliver a sort of pleasure that's somehow both soothing and earth-shattering.

His mouth moves restlessly over mine, one hand on the back of my head, the other pressed between my shoulder blades, holding me close.

"I've missed this," he murmurs, his lips gliding under my chin, nuzzling my jaw. "I've missed you."

His words send a thrill through me, and though I'm not brave enough to say them back out loud, I've missed him, too. I show it as best I can, my head dropping back to give him full access to me, my back arching into him.

"Where'd you get this awful sweater?" he murmurs, pulling the thick turtleneck to better get at my neck.

"Thought you could use a challenge. Builds character," I say a little breathlessly as his warm hands slip beneath the sweater.

"Right. As though you haven't been a challenge from the very beginning."

He gently pushes me back on the couch and moves down my body, shoving the sweater upward and pressing a kiss just below my belly button. He scrapes lightly with his teeth, and I moan.

He presses soft kisses along my rib cage as the sweater inches higher still, and I hear him groan at the realization I ditched the bra when I changed my clothes. He kisses the undersides of my breasts, lingering there until my fingers knot in his hair.

Rough hands shove the sweater higher, his tongue dragging slowly over my nipple before taking it in his mouth. He palms my other breast, kneading firmly in the way he's learned over the years that I like.

My turn.

I push at his shoulders, trying to wiggle out from beneath to get on top, but he refuses to budge, his lips and tongue relentless.

"Matt," I moan. He presses a kiss to the valley between my breasts, and I feel him smile in victory.

"I like when you say my name, especially when you're half-naked."

"I'm not half-naked yet," I argue, trying to get the upper hand however I can.

"Excellent point," he says. He pulls me up, then tugs the sweater over my head and throws it aside. "Much better."

It's the opening I need to get my hands on him, but the second they find his chest, his fingers wrap around my shoulders, easing me back to the couch.

He slides down my body, lips and hands not missing a single erogenous zone as I squirm beneath him.

His fingers hook into the waistband of my yoga pants, his eyes holding mine as he tugs both those and my underwear down my legs. My socks come off with the pants, and he tosses the last of my clothes aside.

His eyes are dark as they look over every inch of me, and my breath catches with want and the unexpected vulnerability of being completely naked in front of him while he's still fully clothed.

I start to sit up, but he places a hand against my stomach as he lowers to his knees beside the couch.

His mouth is warm on the inside of my calf, his fingers insistent, demanding my thighs part as his lips skim up my leg.

The first touch of his tongue nearly undoes me, but he's not done. Not even close. He takes his time, savoring me with long licks and teasing flicks until my fingers are tangled in his hair, silently begging him for release.

As with everything between us, though, sex is a war, and Matt's determined to win this battle.

"Tell me," he murmurs, pulling back slightly. "Tell me what you want."

I stay silent, and he pulls back another inch. "Come on," he teases, only his breath touching me.

I bite my lip and arch into him, trying to bring his mouth closer, but his hand spreads low over my belly, holding me still. He gives me a light lick, and I cry out. So close . . .

"Tell me," he urges, his voice rougher now. "Let me know you want it to be me, love."

It's the unexpected endearment that unravels me—the vulnerability of it lets *me* be vulnerable. I run my fingers softly through his hair and hold his gaze. "Matt."

He closes his eyes on a groan, and this time when he puts his mouth on me it's with purpose. He presses his tongue to me, circling with gentle insistence, knowing exactly what I need.

A sharp cry slips out as I let go—a surprise, since I'm usually more of a silent type.

Matt's hands and mouth gentle as I come down from my orgasm, his touch light and soothing.

I push myself to a seated position as he stands, even as my limbs feel heavy and sated.

I start to reach for him, but he gently grabs both hands. "You don't have to."

I frown in puzzlement. Matt's always been a generous lover, but normally by now he'd be on top of me. Inside me.

He smiles and catches my chin. "I just meant that I wanted to do that. Not because I wanted anything in return. Because I wanted you."

The words are a rush. "Noted. And appreciated. But don't even think about being greedy, Mr. Cannon." I reach for his belt buckle. "Because I want you, too."

Matt's eyes darken with desire, and together we shed his clothes in record time.

I mean to suggest we move to the bedroom, but he's already lowering over me.

His hands are rough and needy as he pulls a condom from his wallet, then spreads my legs. His erection is hot and hard as he nudges me.

Matt lets out a groan and nips my shoulder before lifting his head and locking eyes with mine. "I need you. Now."

I cup his face with my hands, spreading my legs wider in invitation.

His lips capture mine at the precise moment he thrusts inside me, and I gasp against his mouth.

"Damn you," he whispers hoarsely. "Damn you for what you do to me."

Back at you.

My hands move over his broad back, my hips meeting his every thrust.

He kisses me, and I forget everything. Our messy past, his parents, the stupid contract, the fighting. There's only him, only us.

Matt hooks an arm behind my knee, changing the angle just slightly so that every thrust hits me just right.

I cling to his shoulders, my nails digging in in warning.

"Come," he growls against my throat. "Come again."

I do, and he comes with me, our cries unapologetically echoing throughout the quiet living room.

We catch our breath together, neither moving or saying a word. Thank God. I'm not sure there's anything to say.

I'm both dismayed and relieved when the moment's realized by Juno, who comes back into the living room and shoves her rabbit squeaky toy against Matt's hip.

Matt chuckles and gently pushes the dog's face away, which only makes Juno more insistent.

"All right, all right, you win," Matt says, pulling away and standing up. "I knew there was a reason we usually do this at my place."

Actually, the reason we usually "do this" at his place is because it feels safer. Having him in my home is unnerving enough. Having him naked in my home is a whole other thing entirely.

We both gather up our clothes, not meeting each other's eyes as we get dressed.

"Okay," Matt mutters to the dog as he zips his pants. "Now I can play with your damn toy." He winces as he pulls the bunny from Juno's snout.

"Yeah, they get a little . . . slobbery," I say as he tosses the rabbit across the living room, to Juno's delight.

He smiles and wipes his palm against his pant leg, but Juno returns with the toy for another round. Matt repeats the process, playing fetch with my dog's disgusting toy as though it's the most natural thing in the world.

He picks up the abandoned tea and winces as he takes a sip. "I hate tea."

"But you stayed for a cup."

He smiles. "I did, didn't I."

I swallow, wanting to know what it means but too scared to ask. "You want something else to drink?" I say instead.

Matt grins. "You asking me to stay?"

My heart lurches at the question, at what it means. I don't do this sort of thing. I don't ask men to stay for tea and sex and *lingering*.

And yet here I am, wanting desperately for him to stick around, even as I'm terrified he'll say no.

"I'm asking if you want a drink," I dodge.

He grins cockily. "No, you're asking if I want to stay."

I look away.

"Sabrina."

"What?" I snap.

He waits until I relent and meet his eyes. Then he smiles, softer this time. "I'd like to. Stay, I mean."

I shrug as though it's no big deal and doesn't matter to me one way or the other.

But it matters. A lot.

And I'm pretty sure he knows it.

23

Matt

Monday Afternoon, October 2

I don't know what the hell is wrong with me.

I'm sitting across the table from a billionaire who's contemplating giving me free rein to his money. And instead of visualizing the moment of victory when I get Jarod Lanham's business, I'm visualizing him. And Sabrina.

As a couple.

The image is bitter as hell, and yet I can't get it out of my head. Because not only is Lanham richer than hell, he's also . . . decent.

And decent-looking. I've never really given two shits about whether women consider another man attractive. Sure, I'm vaguely aware that Ian and Kennedy are good-looking guys. And that Wolfe's chief technology officer, Dan, looks like a mushroom. But generally speaking, I'm secure enough in my own appeal to the opposite sex not to worry about the competition.

And yet, as I sit here, waiting for Lanham to finish being schmoozed by some corporate goon who ambled over to interrupt our lunch, a guy whose name I've already forgotten, I find my attention's not on my sell.

It's not on the overpriced Kobe burger I've barely touched. Instead, I'm looking at Lanham, trying to figure out if he's Sabrina's type.

Which is bullshit. Sabrina doesn't have a type. Does she?

It bothers me that I don't know.

What I *do* know is the way Lanham was looking at Sabrina last week at lunch, and later at the bar. He'd been a man who saw something he wanted—*her*.

And for her part, Sabrina had seemed . . . *intrigued*.

I take a sip of my drink, studying him from a woman's point of view. From Sabrina's.

Damn it. No way around it, the man's tall, dark, handsome, and absurdly rich.

No, not rich. *I'm* rich. Jarod Lanham is overwhelmingly, couldn't-spend-all-his-money-if-he-wanted-to wealthy.

Not that Sabrina cares about that. I don't know the details of her financial situation, but from what I can tell, she's plenty comfortable. Her apartment, while small, is in a luxury building, and I've never seen her hesitate buying anything she wants, whether it be a new handbag or an expensive glass of wine.

Or high-end clothes. But *those*, of course, she simply put on my bill. I didn't mind. But Lanham *really* wouldn't mind. Hell, he could have bought her the entire store if he felt like it.

The man who's been talking Lanham's ear off apparently realizes he's overstayed his welcome and shakes both our hands in farewell before returning to his table.

Lanham smiles in apology. "Sorry about that. I barely know the guy, but he seems to think we go way back."

"No problem." I take a half-hearted bite of my burger; he takes a more enthusiastic forkful of his salad.

I'm about to dive into my assessment of his current portfolio, which I spent half the night reviewing, when he speaks first.

"You from here, Cannon?"

"Sort of. I grew up in Connecticut, but my dad worked here in the city. We'd come into Manhattan for the usual things—Broadway shows, the tree at Rockefeller Center during the holidays, the Macy's Thanksgiving Day Parade."

I don't tell him that at about half those events, it had been my dad and Felicia who'd brought me, not my dad and mom. Not because my mom wasn't all about the New York stuff but because it gave her an opportunity to spend the day with her flavor of the month. Because that's the sort of fucked-up thing my parents did that was okay in the name of "modern parenting."

"Never done any of that," he says, lifting his glass of red wine and swishing it thoughtfully. "Think I'd like to."

"It's overrated." I pick up a fry, cram it into my mouth. "The parade's crazy, the tree's the same damn thing every year, and don't even get me started on musicals."

He gives a slight smile. "You're awfully cynical of your city."

"None of that's my city," I say emphatically. "Not the real city. We New Yorkers may be used to the touristy stuff the same way we are used to the chaos of Times Square or the exorbitant price to get to the top of the Empire State Building. But the heart of the city is its people, not the famous places or events."

Lanham thinks on this a moment, then nods in approval and sips his wine. "I like that. Hell, I like the city."

I eat another fry, watching him. "You contemplating a move?"

"I am."

Huh. Normally I'd be thrilled. If he signs on as a client, and that's still a *big* if, his local status would make my job easier. Easier to meet with him in person to discuss strategy, easier to schmooze him and keep him happy so that his money stays with Wolfe.

Now, however, I can't help but wonder if his reasons for staying have something to do with some*one.*

I mentally slap myself for being ridiculous. He's met Sabrina twice, and one of those encounters had lasted fewer than five minutes.

He sets his wineglass back on the table and pushes away his salad plate. Arms on the table, he leans forward slightly, his expression intent. "Let me ask you something."

"Sure." I push aside thoughts of Sabrina, forcing myself to focus on my job. On saying the right things to land this dude already.

"If I sign with you . . ."

My pulse thrums with anticipation.

"Does that mean your bosses will get off your back about the Vegas shit?"

I manage to keep myself from tensing, but barely. "Sorry?"

He smiles. "Come on. You're telling me they didn't ride you hard about damaging company brand after getting caught with a hooker and coke?"

"It was a mediocre lap dance, and I don't touch the hard stuff," I say through gritted teeth.

"I believe you," he says in a quiet, no-BS tone that tells me he means it. "But I also know that this business, hell, *most* businesses, run on reputation. You can't tell me your bosses didn't shit themselves in panic and threaten to send you to rehab."

I lift my drink and say nothing.

He leans forward even more. "You didn't go to rehab, but you did the next-best thing. You got yourself a gorgeous woman to stand by your side and dilute your playboy reputation."

My eyes narrow in warning, and Lanham holds up his hands in a placating motion. "No judgment. I'd do the same thing. Hell, I *have* done the same thing. People love a good playboy, but they'll turn on you just as fast if you take it too far. You're smart to hitch your wagon to Sabrina's."

I maintain my silence, but he doesn't let it drop.

"You guys serious?"

Again, I try to maintain my silence, but my irritation slips out. "Why all the interest?"

"You didn't answer the question."

"Yeah," I snap. "We're serious."

He studies me, then nods and resumes eating. "All right."

"That's not the answer you wanted, is it?" I say.

He shrugs. "Sabrina's very compelling. But I don't make moves on another man's woman."

I grit my teeth. *Sabrina's very compelling.* Damn straight she is. And I don't believe for one second that this billionaire wouldn't make a move the moment the opportunity presented itself.

"So, are there wedding bells in your future?"

I resist the urge to grab his fork and stab him with it. "People can be committed without being married."

Lanham lifts a shoulder.

"You don't think so?" I ask, ignoring the fact that of all the conversations I've ever pictured having with Jarod Lanham, this isn't one of them.

He sits back in his chair and looks at me. "Call me old-fashioned, but I like the idea of a man and woman committing to each other. One person. With vows."

I'm careful to hide my surprise. The Jarod Lanham I've seen in tabloids hardly seems the marrying type. He's had girlfriends, sure, but he's had a lot of them. Back-to-back. Nothing about the guy has ever indicated he wants to settle down.

He gives a rueful smile. "You don't agree?"

I shrug and keep my answer deliberately vague, since I barely know the guy. "Doesn't matter if I do or not. It's your life. You want to walk down the aisle and spend a fortune on a wedding, that's your business."

Lanham shakes his head. "It's not about the wedding. It's about what comes after. I don't give a shit about being a fiancé, but I wouldn't mind waking up to the same face every morning. Having someone to share my life with. A companion."

The words are so familiar, I think for a moment I'm experiencing déjà vu, and then it hits me. I have had this conversation before, but not with Lanham. With Sabrina.

His thoughts on marriage mirror hers almost exactly.

The realization makes me want to punch something. Because of how compatible they are. Because she doesn't actually belong to me . . .

"Sorry," Lanham says, shaking his head. "You're probably wondering why the hell I'm talking about my personal life instead of my portfolio."

His statement jolts me back to the present, and I'm more than a little annoyed to discover that . . .

I *hadn't* been wondering that.

Despite having spent most of my career prepping to get in front of someone with this guy's money, I'm not nearly as excited as I thought I'd be. For some reason, it just doesn't feel as important as I thought it would.

I hear myself going through my pitch with Lanham, discussing my strategy for his portfolio and reciting all the reasons why he'd be a fool not to sign with me, but all I can think is that this—my job—is no longer the most vital thing in my life.

The realization is terrifying.

24

Sabrina

Wednesday Evening, October 4

“If you tell me this is homemade, we can’t be friends anymore,” I say, scooping up a glob of delicious white cheese and plopping it onto toasted sourdough.

Lara snags an olive with one hand, refills our wineglasses with the other. “If by homemade, you mean did I open the container of burrata, put it on the plate, and put olive oil and salt on top? Yep, totally homemade. I also popped that bread right in the toaster, like a Food Network boss.”

“I freaking love burrata,” Kate says, happily chewing her own piece of bread. “And wine. And you guys.”

I give her a look out of the corner of my eye. “How much wine has she had?” I ask Lara good-naturedly.

“Just the one glass. But she’s been like this ever since she got here. I think she’s in love.”

“The only thing I’m in love with is cheese,” Kate retorts.

I lick burrata off my thumb, not entirely sure I believe her, but I suppose it’s possible. It’s hard not to be in love with cheese.

"So, is this going to be like a thing?" Kate asks, resting her elbows on Lara and Ian's kitchen counter. "You guys hosting spontaneous dinner parties? Because I sort of love it."

Lara pushes her glasses up on her nose. "You know, I sort of love it, too." She smiles, as though surprised by the realization. "Who'd have thought that a former SEC agent would be hosting some of Wall Street's elite in my swanky apartment?"

"I'm *almost* jealous of the fab apartment, but you have to put up with Ian, and I don't know that I could," Kate says, sipping her wine.

"You do that all day long," I point out.

"Nope. Different," Kate says. "The guys are totally different in their work habitat."

"How's that?" Kennedy says, ambling into the kitchen.

"Thought you were having man talk on the balcony," I say, tilting my head back toward the glass doors off Ian's living room that lead to a small outdoor space with a hell of a view.

"We are, but . . ." He holds up his empty wineglass as explanation for why he's in the kitchen, then reaches for a bottle of red on the counter. "Besides, this is far more interesting. How are we different in the office?" he asks Kate again.

Kate pushes a strand of straight dark hair behind her ear, but it promptly falls forward again, quietly stubborn, much like the head it belongs to. "I'll clarify. Ian and Matt are different inside the office. You're more of the same."

"Yeah?" He takes a sip of wine and watches her. "Explain."

"No thanks."

"Explain," he repeats.

"See, this is exactly what I mean," Kate says testily. "You're bossy in the office, bossy outside the office . . ."

"And you're not?"

"It's my job to be bossy. Someone has to make sure you guys keep your pants zipped up so you don't go thinking with your . . ." Kate gestures in the vicinity of Kennedy's crotch, and Lara chokes into her wine.

Kennedy's eyebrows lift. "Wasn't aware that my"—he, too, gestures to his crotch—"was any of my assistant's business."

Her cheeks color slightly. "It's not. Obviously. Neither is Ian's or Matt's. But while we're on the subject . . ."

Kate gives me a sly look, and I give her a mental salute of respect for the skillful change of subject. Still, I can respect her without playing along. "Not open for discussion."

"Oh, come on," Lara says. "What the heck is going on with you guys? You've been in the same general area for nearly half an hour, and there hasn't been a single fight."

"Well, one of them's been on the balcony, the other in the kitchen," Kennedy points out. "It'd be hard to fight across that distance, even for them."

"Shush," Lara says. "Don't ruin this for me. I want the scoop."

"You already know the scoop." I take a sip of my Chardonnay. "We have an arrangement. I play his doting girlfriend when needed and make the world believe he's done with his partying ways."

"I think it's working," Kate says. "Your morning coffee dates have all the women around the office talking. The general vibe is disappointment that Matt's off the market, not skepticism that it's a ploy."

"Ian and I ran into an old colleague of the guys' at dinner the other night," Lara chimes in. "His wife was sweet but a total gossip hound, and she was relentless about finding out if a ring's in your future after they saw you 'making love eyes' across the table at each other."

I wince. "Damn. We might be doing our job a little too well."

"Or maybe not," Kennedy says with his usual storm-cloud touch. "Jarod Lanham's not buying it."

I frown. "What do you mean?"

"Rumor has it he's *very* interested in whatever you and Matt have going on."

I freeze. *What?*

Frantically, my brain goes back to Jarod's and my conversation at the bar that first night. Had I slipped up somehow? Inadvertently let him on to our ruse . . . ?

Kennedy freezes midsip, looking atypically nonplussed. "Matt didn't tell you?"

"Tell me what? And don't say *nothing*," I say, lifting a finger in warning.

"You're just like Kate when you're pissed." Kennedy sighs. "Matt and Lanham had lunch on Monday. Matt said he was fishing for info on your relationship. I thought you knew."

No, I didn't know.

I've barely talked to Matt after our marathon sex weekend. Apparently when I'm not needed for sex or fake relationships, he has no use for me.

Lara pushes the cheese board toward me. "Eat this, sweetie."

"And have a sip of this," Kate says, picking up my wineglass and holding it up to my mouth.

I let out a little laugh. "I'm not mad."

"You look a little mad," Kennedy says into his glass.

"No, I'm just . . ."

Hurt.

"Concerned," I finish. "I can't do my job if Matt doesn't give me all the information."

"I will say, his schedule's been crazy," Kate says kindly. "He's barely had a free minute between meetings."

The balcony door opens, and the sound of male laughter fills the air as Ian and Matt step back into the living room.

I'm already off the barstool, wineglass in hand, as I stomp toward them.

Ian gives me a wide-eyed look. "Don't hurt me."

I ignore him and, putting a palm on Matt's chest, push him back onto the balcony. "You and me, outside."

Matt gives me a slightly amused look. "Can I at least get another drink first?"

My only response to that is to shut the door on the rest of the group so it's just the two of us, forty-something stories above Manhattan.

Too late, I realize my mistake. It's *cold* out here. The guys all came from work, and their suit jackets are enough to protect them from the worst of the fall air. My thin blouse? Not so much.

"Why do you look ready to cut someone?" Matt asks, shrugging out of his jacket and handing it to me.

I ignore the jacket. "Did you meet with Jarod Lanham on Monday?"

He goes still for a moment, then steps toward me, wrapping his coat around my shoulders when I make no effort to take it myself. "Yes."

"Why didn't you tell me?"

"I was getting around to it," he says simply.

I pull his coat closer around me. "But you told Kennedy first."

Matt tilts his head curiously. "Sure. I work with the guys. I see them all day, every day."

"Yeah, but we're . . ."

He steps closer, starting to grin, even as his gaze grows sharper. "We're what?"

I blow out an irritated breath. "We're . . . colleagues. Of a sort. Not like you and the guys, but—"

He dips his head and kisses me. Not like he wants to shut me up, not like he's trying to win an argument, but because he wants to.

I stubbornly keep my lips closed, my stance stiff, but he's just as stubborn. His lips brush over mine, gently but insistently, his hands slipping inside his jacket to rest on my waist.

Matt's kiss is all the more compelling for its tenderness, his touch more convincing for its patience. His tongue gently touches the center of my bottom lip, and I relent with a sigh, opening my mouth to his, lifting my arms to wrap around his neck.

His jacket slips off, but neither of us notices. He wraps his arms all the way around me, tilting his head, and I forget all about the autumn chill, Jarod Lanham, even our friends just on the other side of the glass doors.

My eyes fly open. *Glass* doors . . .

I pull back and whip my head around. Sure enough, all four of our friends are watching us unabashedly. Lara and Kate are grinning outright. Even crusty Kennedy seems amused.

But my eyes lock with Ian's. The guy's my best friend, and I know him well enough to know when he's concerned.

About me?

Or for Matt?

I want to tell him that he doesn't need to worry. That even though we're full-on playing with fire, we won't get burned. Our hearts are damn near inflammable.

I feel Matt's right hand move and glance down to see him giving our friends the finger. A laugh bubbles out of me, and I'm surprised at how girlish and happy it sounds.

Our friends laugh and take the hint, moving away from the windowed door. Most of them do, anyway. Ian lingers a bit longer, his smile tight until Lara whispers something in his ear that makes him smile for real.

Matt brings my attention back to him, setting a palm to the side of my cheek. "About my lunch with Lanham . . ."

"Yeah?"

"I don't know." His brow furrows. "I got the feeling he was more interested than he should be in the status of our relationship."

"And that bothers you?"

He gives a slight smile. "Turns out I might be the jealous type."

"Even when it's just a fake girlfriend?" I say, keeping my voice teasing to hide my thrill at the thought of Matt being possessive. Of me.

"Apparently," he murmurs before taking a deep breath. "I need to ask another favor."

I smile. "If it's dinner with your parents again, you better have some more flowers."

He blows out a breath. "It might be worse. It's about Lanham. And our . . . arrangement."

"Okay . . ."

"He's close to signing," Matt says, sounding more indifferent than I'd have expected. "I wasn't sure, because our meeting on Monday seemed more like a battle of wills than anything else. But The Sams called me into their office today and said that he's narrowed it down to me and a senior director from Schmitt and Sons."

"Damn," I mutter. "Schmitt's the best in the business."

He gives me a look, and I pat his chest reassuringly. "Besides Wolfe, of course."

"The Sams are more intent than ever that I don't mess this up for them, especially after they found out that the Schmitt guys pulled out all the stops with a trip to Newport last weekend."

"Who's the broker?" I ask.

"Jeff Goldberg."

I groan.

Let me put it this way: Jeff Goldberg's the type of man who will never need my services. He'd never need reputation repair, a fake girlfriend, help burying secrets, legal representation, nothing.

The guy married his childhood sweetheart. Not high school sweetheart. *Childhood.* They met in first grade. They have five kids, all prep-school darlings. An enormous apartment overlooking Central Park. A freaking Golden Retriever.

"Thanks for the vote of confidence," Matt says with a laugh. "But you see why my bosses are freaking out."

"What do you need?"

"The Sams have a place in the Hamptons. Five bedrooms, right on the water. It's off-season. They invited us to join them, along with Lanham and a guest, for a weekend getaway."

"Part of your redemption plan?"

"Probably."

"You think it'll help?"

He sighs. "I don't know. It can't hurt. I'd like to think things are getting better, but I can tell some of my more conservative clients are still jumpy. And The Sams definitely are."

The agony on his face is real, and I know that the reality of his Vegas shenanigans is hitting him harder than ever. And though some deep instinct tells me I'm likely to regret it, I hear myself agreeing to the trip.

He closes his eyes in relief. "Thank you. You good to leave Friday morning?"

"Sure. Are we taking your car?"

"Yeah, I thought we could get up there first, get settled into our domestic-bliss mode for the weekend. Everyone else is coming later."

"Sounds good. I'll see if Kate can stay with Juno."

Matt shrugs. "Bring her."

"I can't bring a dog to your bosses' place in the Hamptons!"

"Why not? She'll love the beach. She's house-trained. And nothing says 'settled down' like a dog."

"True." The thought of a weekend getaway with Matt *and* Juno is admittedly appealing. "So, which version of 'settled down' are we going for this weekend? Same as we've been doing, acting delightfully smitten with each other? Or are we going for broke and selling it *hard*, dropping lots of 'we' as it relates to our future and talking about ring shopping?"

Matt's wince is subtle. So subtle that if I hadn't been watching for it, I might have missed it. But I *was* watching for it.

Given what I know, I was fully expecting words like *future* and *ring shopping* to be the thing to send a guy like Matt Cannon running for the hills.

What I'm *not* expecting is how much his flinch stings.

"Let's see how it goes," he says. "I'm guessing some hand-holding and pet names will be enough to convince everyone that I've given up my lap-dance ways."

"Okay." My tone is agreeable, but his eyes narrow on me slightly.

"You don't agree?"

"I—" I bite my lip, knowing I need to tread carefully.

The truth is, something feels off. Jarod Lanham seems more interested in Matt and my relationship, as well as my skills as a potential matchmaker, than he does hiring Matt as his broker. Even more perplexing, Matt doesn't seem to care nearly as much as he should, considering the opinion of people like Jarod is the reason Matt and I started this charade in the first place.

As for me . . . I *do* care. I care about all of this. A little too much.

He rubs a hand over the back of his neck. "This whole thing has gotten rather fucked, hasn't it?"

I laugh, not so much with mirth but with dismay that he seems to be reading my thoughts. "It'll work out," I say, smiling to help sell what feels like a lie.

If I can't get my weird feelings and this strange sense of doom under control, it won't work out at all.

He looks away without saying anything, and after a too-long silence, I touch his arm. "You want Jarod Lanham as a client, don't you?"

He hesitates only a moment before nodding. "Yeah."

"Then let's play our part and get you your man." I keep my voice light and start to turn away.

He grabs my wrist. "Sabrina, are you going with me because of the contract?"

"Are you asking me to go because of the contract?" I counter.

The door opens, and Kate's head pops out. "Guys. I ate all the cheese, and they won't let me have anything else until you join us. And I'm *starving.*"

"Be right there," I say, dragging my gaze away from Matt's.

I start to pull back, and his fingers tighten for a moment on my wrist before he slowly releases me.

As we go inside, I realize that neither of us answered the question.

Are we going to the Hamptons together because of the contract?

Or in spite of it?

25

Matt

Friday Afternoon, October 6

Well. *Shit.*

My weekend just got a hell of a lot more complicated.

Wordlessly, I hold out my phone to Sabrina so she can see the text message that's just come through.

We're standing in The Sams' kitchen at their place in the Hamptons, sipping a glass of champagne to kick off what we'd expected to be a long weekend of make-believe in front of two bosses and a billionaire.

Instead, I'm bracing for Sabrina's irritation as she silently reads the text.

She hands the phone back to me and takes a sip of champagne. "Well. I guess that means I don't need to freak out about the fact that Juno's already put her muddy paws all over the duvet in the master bedroom."

"I can't believe they canceled," I say, still distracted by the message from Samantha. "Who the hell does that?"

"Maybe they thought they were doing you a favor," she says, going to the fridge for the champagne bottle. "They probably figured that if the prospective client couldn't come, there was no reason for the four of us to suffer through the awkwardness of small talk."

I ignore her placating. "And what kind of bullshit is 'something came up'? It's the oldest, lamest blow off in the books."

"So you'll woo Jarod some other way," she says, reaching across the counter to top off my glass.

I put a hand out to stop her. "I shouldn't. Not if I'm driving back."

"No way," she says, batting my hand away and refilling the glass. "I am not getting back in the car with that dog just yet."

I laugh at the memory of Juno wailing the entire ride from the Upper East Side to Southampton. "You'd think she'd never been in a car before."

"She probably hasn't," Sabrina pointed out. "I don't own a car. Her vet's within walking distance, so I've never needed to put her in a cab or subway. And I got her from a shelter in Harlem when she was a young puppy."

"Where is the monster, anyway?" I ask, looking around the lavish beach home for the dog.

"Outside. I decided she'd be better off digging a hole in the sand than your bosses' bed."

"She won't run away?"

Sabrina shakes her head and walks to the back door that opens onto the beach. "Watch this."

She lets out a short, no-nonsense whistle, and not thirty seconds later, a wet, sandy dog bounds toward her. Sabrina holds up a hand before the dog can burst inside the house, and Juno plants her butt down on the porch, tail wagging wildly as she waits for praise.

"Good girl," Sabrina says in a voice I've never heard her use before. It's adoring and a little goofy, and I can't help but smile as she squats down to pet her dog.

Sabrina's wearing an expensive-looking red sweater and light-gray slacks, but she doesn't so much as flinch when Juno sets her paws on Sabrina's knee and goes in for a slobbery on-the-cheek kiss.

"Okay, that's plenty of love," Sabrina says after a moment, laughing as she pushes the dog away. "Go continue your beach exploration."

Juno bounds away again, and I give Sabrina an admiring look. "Is there anyone you don't have completely wrapped around your finger, ready to do your bidding with a simple whistle?"

She gives a coy smile. "Well. I'm still working on you."

I'm not so sure. Every time I'm with her—hell, every time I look at her—it becomes harder and harder to think about going back to the way we were.

For the first time, I truly understand why Sabrina put her no-hookup rule into place. And though I don't regret violating the rule in every pleasurable way possible in recent days, I'm no longer entirely confident in what we're doing. Or why we're doing it.

I should be dying to get back to the city, back to my real life, now that Lanham and my bosses have canceled, but instead, *this* is what feels real. The thought is both compelling and terrifying.

"So, how long does she need?" I ask, nodding to where Juno disappeared. "I'd like to start back before it gets dark."

Her glass pauses halfway to her lips, and her eyes reflect disappointment, though she responds with her usual tart sass. "Damn, you really have gotten old. Don't worry, Grandpa. We'll get you home before supper."

"I'm just saying, if there's nobody here—"

"Right, I get it. No point in putting on the show with no audience," she interrupts. "I wrote the contract, remember?"

"Sabrina."

She sets her champagne on the kitchen table. "I'm going to take a quick walk. I'll call Juno in on my way back, and we can get going as soon as I get her cleaned up."

I grit my teeth. I know her well enough to know she'll walk out the door no matter what I say, so I stay silent and let her go.

I start to sip my champagne, but I no longer want it. I set it aside and pull a beer out of the fridge instead. Popping the cap, I wander out onto the porch, scanning the beach until I see Sabrina's slim figure in the red sweater, the big dog running long laps around her with a huge stick extending on either side of her head.

For a painful moment, I feel a fierce longing to join them. To be welcome to join them.

Instead, I sip my beer and take in a long breath of salty ocean air.

It's nice. Nicer than I realized, to get out of the city, where I don't feel the constant need to check email, to answer my phone, to straighten my tie, to be quick with a joke.

It's even a relief to have a break from the numbers. That's the thing with this damn calculator brain of mine. If numbers are there, I process them, even when I don't need to. Everything from the stock ticker on every TV in Wall Street down to the receipt at a restaurant sets the numbers part of my brain humming.

Much in the way I imagine writers always have a little part of their attention tapped into their next story, a little part of me seems to be sorting and re-sorting numbers, just because they're there.

But they're not here now. There's nothing but afternoon sunshine, a brisk breeze, sand, water . . . a beautiful woman.

My woman.

It's past time I do something about that.

Hell if I know what. Or how.

I go back into the kitchen and open the fridge, this time to survey the food situation. Not only did The Sams have a whole arsenal of gourmet groceries delivered by some fancy white-glove service, they'd been planning on a party of six for the entire weekend.

The food options are endless. My cooking skills? Not so much.

I pull out a couple of varieties of expensive cheese and an enormous New York strip steak. This I can handle. Probably. I also find a couple of baking potatoes and crackers from the pantry and a serving dish to put the cheese on.

A few minutes later, I've got a decent-looking cheese plate happening, potatoes in the oven, and red wine decanting on the counter. My steak-seasoning skills are limited to salt and pepper, but gauging from the price tag on the steak, I don't think it'll matter so long as I don't burn the hell out of it.

I've just turned on the grill on the back porch when I hear Juno's bark, followed by the dog's awkward scampering up the stairs. A moment later, Sabrina appears.

She freezes when she sees me, and I freeze, too, not in surprise, but because of how beautiful she looks. The wind and sea air have made her hair wilder and wavier than usual, and her cheeks are flushed pink, not from any expensive compact but from the wind, and because I know her . . . probably from a little anger. At me.

Her gaze flits from my face to the grill lid that's still open, then down at the dog, who must have some sort of sixth sense that meat is on the horizon because she's panting happily, her tail wagging like crazy.

I clear my throat. "Figured it was a waste to go back tonight. After we drove all the way here."

She leans against one of the pillars of the porch, crossing her arms. "It's a big house to have all to ourselves."

Juno barks in objection at being left out, but we both ignore her.

I slowly walk toward Sabrina. "I'm doing it for you, you know. As good as your professional skills are, your domestic persona's a little rusty."

Her eyebrows lift. "Is that so?"

"Don't get me wrong, you do sushi restaurants and cocktail parties really well. And museum fund-raisers, and dinner parties, and dresses and heels."

"Why do I get the sense I'm being insulted somehow?"

"Because it's me," I say, reaching out and capturing an errant curl, just because I can. "And because it's you. And because over the years you've built up so many damn walls where I'm concerned, you won't hear a damn thing I say without first filtering it for an insult."

"Maybe that's because that's how you started out this whole thing."

"Or maybe," I say quietly, "it's because even then you were primed to be suspicious."

Her nostrils flare in irritation. "Just like a man, putting the blame on me. Poor you, wrongfully accused—"

"No, *rightly* accused," I interrupt. "I don't deny that I was an idiot. But maybe you got my motivations wrong."

"Meaning?"

"Meaning I have walls, too. And back on that first night, I think I was terrified that, for the first time in my adult life, someone might scale them. That *you* might scale them."

Her lips part in surprise, but for once, she has no sassy retort. Instead she studies me for a long moment. "If we stay, I'm not helping cook."

"Well thank God for that," I say, playing along with her need to lighten the mood.

Sabrina smiles, then reaches out and grabs the beer from my hand, taking a sip. Then she makes a face. "I hate beer."

"Wine's open in the kitchen."

"Much better," she says. "You fetch that while I take Juno around to the hose on the side of the house. Though I'm not sure wet dog will be that much better than sandy dog."

She heads back down the steps, whistling for Juno to follow, and I allow myself a small smile. I know that I've just lost a prime opportunity to spend time wooing a richer-than-shit dream client.

But I'm not the least bit upset by it.

Because instead, I get an entire weekend to go about wooing my dream woman.

26

Sabrina

Friday Night, October 6

After the sun set, the weather went quickly from being "brisk and refreshing" to downright cold, but neither Matt nor I seemed to care. Instead we pulled on every layer we brought with us, helped ourselves to the stack of fleece blankets rolled neatly in a basket by the back door, and curled up on the enormous padded chaise longue overlooking the water.

Juno's sprawled out at our feet, finally tired from her endless laps on the beach, and even with the zap of bugs against the porch light and the occasional rowdy laughter from a group of teens farther up the beach, the night's the most peaceful I've experienced in a long time.

"More wine?" Matt asks, glancing down to where I have my wineglass propped up on his knee, my head on his shoulder.

"Nah, I'm good. You?"

"Saving room for dessert."

I groan. "I can't even think about having more food. That steak was enormous, and you put half a stick of butter on my potato."

"It's the only way to eat the things. That or fried."

"Or mashed," I point out.

"I never liked mashed potatoes," he muses. "I think because they remind me of Thanksgiving."

I lift my head to look at him. "You don't like Thanksgiving?"

He grins. "You've met my parents. What do you think?"

"Tell me Felicia didn't come over for holidays."

"Not until I was in college. I guess they figured with me gone most of the time, there was no point in keeping up pretenses anymore. Not that they ever did a good job of that in the first place."

"God, you poor kid," I murmur.

"It wasn't so bad."

"It was pretty bad," I say with a laugh.

He looks at me, his eyes going serious. "Yours was worse."

I suck in a quick breath. "You know, maybe I will grab some more wine."

I start to stand, but he puts a hand on my leg, holding me still. "Sabrina."

"What?"

"Why don't you ever talk about your childhood, your life before New York?"

"Because it sucked. As you've already said, yours was bad; mine was worse. I don't see the point in discussing things best left in the distant past. Ian's the only thing from that part of my life that's still around."

He flinches. It's slight, almost imperceptible, but enough to give me pause. Surely Matt's not jealous of Ian. Is he?

"I didn't mean to imply . . . I just . . . I didn't even know you then."

"I know. Which is why it sucks that I'm always on the outside, like I'm being punished for growing up in Connecticut instead of Philadelphia with you two."

I touch his arm. "That's not what this is about. This isn't me trusting Ian more than you."

"Okay," he says quietly, and my chest clenches in panic. He's giving up on me already. I should be relieved. Instead, I feel . . . lost.

"It's fine, Sabrina." Matt's blue eyes soften as his touch moves from my knee to my cheek. "You don't have to tell me." The gentle tenderness in his voice is like a battering ram on the very walls he mentioned earlier in the evening.

My self-preservation's stayed strong for years, but my need to keep everything compartmentalized into painful past and carefully restrained present seems to be wavering a little more with every passing day. First with Lara and Kate, now with him.

Especially with him.

Maybe it's time. Maybe it's past time.

I take a breath for courage. "It's not a pretty story."

His eyes widen in surprise. Then he wordlessly hands me his whiskey, which is stronger than my wine. I smile and take a sip. I'm not above using liquid courage.

"It's not a long story, either," I say, handing him back his glass. "I mean, it's not like some convoluted saga."

"Damn, I love those. All guys do."

I smile at his sarcasm, using it to buy some time as I pluck at a stray string on the blanket.

He stays silent, waiting for me. Letting me do it my way when I'm ready.

"So. You know I grew up in Philly. But it wasn't like Liberty Bell, cheesesteak-sandwich-wars Philadelphia. We're talking a neighborhood you've never heard of, or, if you have, it's because of its crime rates."

I pull harder on the string.

"My dad died when I was a baby. Heroin overdose. Though, from what I was able to piece together about him when I got older, I'm not sure he'd have been around if he'd lived. Sexual assault record, vehicular manslaughter . . . all sorts of nasty stuff."

The tiny little string I've been fiddling with is now nearly a foot long, courtesy of my nerves. Matt puts his hand on mine, linking our fingers, and squeezes. *Continue.*

"It was just my mom and me for a while. Then later, my two half brothers lived with us. We alternated between crappy housing and crappy trailers. I'm not sure I ever lived in one place longer than a year. She liked her drugs a little bit, her booze a lot. But mostly?" I take a breath. "Mostly she liked her men. Or maybe the men liked her."

"What's she look like?"

It's an easy question, and I suspect he means it to be. I squeeze his hand. "Like me. Brown eyes instead of blue, but otherwise I look just like her."

What I don't say out loud is that every time I glance in the mirror, I feel a tiny flash of fear that the similarities are inside as well as out. That I'm just as cold, opportunistic, and self-absorbed.

"So she was beautiful. What else?"

"You're good at this," I say begrudgingly.

"Only with you." He brushes a strand of hair off my face.

My heart does something ridiculous, and I look away, knowing that the hard part is still to come.

"She never kept a job for long," I say, my words a little bit rushed. "She worked on and off at clothing stores but got fired for helping herself to the items. Or she'd work at a cheap diner and get fired for being a lot better at flirting with the customers than actually getting them their food."

"How about you? How'd you get your food?"

"Let's just say those Thanksgivings you dreaded? I'd have killed to have my mom even acknowledge it was Thanksgiving."

Matt's fingers squeeze on mine, this time a bit harder. "Damn it, Sabrina."

"It wasn't so bad," I say. "When I got old enough, I figured out that some of the bigger grocery store chains did to-go boxes with turkey and potatoes, the whole thing. I'd save up every penny from my job at a Dunkin' Donuts to buy enough for my brothers and my mom, too, if it was a good year."

"And for yourself?"

I don't answer, because what I need to tell him, what he needs to know, isn't about whether or not I got cranberry sauce as a kid.

"I mentioned my mom liked her men." My words are quiet now, even more rushed. "It was more than that. She used sex to get things she wanted from them."

Matt makes a dismayed, angry noise.

"It took me a while to figure out what was going on. How soon after she'd bring home a guy, we'd have a new TV. Or she'd have new shoes. Or a little more spending money. I'd ask her about it, and she'd laugh and say it was a loan. Or an arrangement. It got worse as she got more and more dependent on 'having nice things,' as she put it. On bad weeks, there was a different man every night. A different arrangement."

"Jesus," he says in a stunned voice, setting aside his glass and dragging his hand over his face. "No wonder you don't like to talk about it."

"Yeah, mentioning that your mom dabbled in barely disguised prostitution doesn't make for great conversation."

He looks back at me, his eyes dark and glittering. "Did she ever ask it of you?"

I suck in a breath that he hit so quickly on the truth. Nobody knows that part of it. Not even Ian.

"Sabrina," he says on a breath.

"Nothing happened," I rush to reassure him, because he looks ready to punch something. "And she didn't ask me, not exactly. But the older I got, the more her men suggested it. My mom said no, but I saw her face, and the reason she said no wasn't due to outrage over a forty-something man touching her daughter. It was jealousy. Competition. She'd never been particularly affectionate, but after that, it felt like an all-out war between us."

I take a sip of my wine.

"I graduated at eighteen, and after basically harassing my half brothers' family to take full custody and give them a stable home, I took the first bus I could out of there."

"You ever go back?"

"Never," I say emphatically.

"You talk to her?"

I hesitate, a little ashamed of my answer. "No. But I send her a birthday gift every year. I don't know why. It only opens the door to guilt trips and requests for money."

He inhales long and hard through his nose, as though searching for the right words. Instead he pulls my wineglass out of my hand, sets it aside. Then he gathers me to him, my head against his chest, his heart steady and reassuring beneath my ear.

I feel his lips on my hair, and though I don't think I've ever sought a hug for comfort in my entire life, at this moment, I get why people do. I let my arm slide around his waist, closing my eyes at how right it feels to be held by him.

Neither of us speaks for long minutes, lost in our own thoughts. Me, relief at finally having my ugly past out there. Him, likely trying to process it all.

"I've got two questions. Not sure you'll like either one," he says finally, breaking the silence.

I smile but don't lift my head. "You sure know how to get a girl excited."

"Your mom's past. Is that why you were so destroyed by my callous words when we first met? When I said you were worth every penny?"

"Whoa, hey now," I say, pushing up to a seated position. "I wasn't destroyed. I was annoyed."

He says nothing, just waits.

I wait, too.

He wins.

"Okay, fine, yes. You struck a nerve, although you obviously didn't do it intentionally."

"Well, even not knowing your past, I shouldn't have said it," he says, running a hand over my hair. "But knowing your past . . . I'd give anything for a time machine."

"To change my childhood or to change that night?"

"Both," he says with a smile.

I smile back. "What's your second question?"

"Are your mom's relationships with men the reason you're anti-relationship?"

"Yes," I say without hesitation. "But to be fair, where I'm from, there weren't many happy relationships. Most of the kids in my class came from divorced homes, single-parent families, foster homes. My school wasn't exactly a quaint little brick building off Main Street."

He winces, and I laugh.

"Oh my gosh. You went to a brick school off Main Street, didn't you?"

"Technically it was Main *Drive*."

"Well . . ." I go back to fiddling with the string on the blanket. "If knowing you has taught me anything, it's that a nice house in a neighborhood with clean streets doesn't always mean a happy home."

"Certainly not," he says in agreement. "But my family issues . . . God, I can't believe I even complained about them to you."

"Don't think that way," I say, looking up and meeting his eyes. "Your pains are just as valid."

We hold each other's gaze for several seconds, and there's nothing uncomfortable about it. Merely understanding.

"We're kind of screwed up, huh?" he says with a sad smile.

"I prefer the word *guarded*." I wink in an effort to lighten the mood. "We're just smart enough to know that two people can enjoy each other's company, maybe even be friends, without the whole messy, painful stuff."

He pushes his hand farther into my hair, fingers tangling in the messy curls. "Friends, huh?"

"Hypothetically. You know, in theory. For people who actually like each other."

"Not us, though," Matt murmurs.

"Definitely not," I say softly as he pulls me in for a kiss, and I smile when I feel his smile.

The kiss starts out light and playful, but with each brush of our lips, we linger a little longer, our breath growing a little faster.

"Sabrina," he says. "This enjoying-each-other's-company thing you speak of . . ."

"Yeah?"

"Care to enjoy each other's company . . ." His mouth moves down my neck. "You care to enjoy each other in the bedroom?"

I manage a nod, and when Matt stands and scoops me into his arms, I have the breathtaking realization that despite my words, I've been wrong about not having avoided the "messy, painful stuff."

I'm horribly, awfully aware that . . . I'm already in the middle of it.

I'm already all the way, painfully in love with a man who will never love me back.

27

Matt

Friday Night, October 6

I thought I knew every type of sex. Fast sex. Playful sex. Angry sex. Dirty sex. Public sex. Vanilla sex . . .

The moment I set Sabrina on the bed, I know tonight is different. I know that whatever's about to happen between us will go beyond anything I've known before.

Because tonight matters. She matters.

And I intend to show her.

Sabrina's hands reach for me the moment I lower over her, but I gently take both her hands in mine, pressing them down to the mattress as my mouth moves over hers.

She huffs in protest but kisses me back, her lips and tongue greedy, her hips tilting toward mine in invitation.

Lifting her hands above her head, I pin her wrists with my left hand and use my right to skim down her side, flattening my palm to her hip. *Slow down. Let me savor you.*

I feel the moment she capitulates, her breath coming out on a sigh against my lips. She tastes a little like wine and whiskey, but mostly she tastes like her. That elusive, captivating element that is simply Sabrina.

No woman has ever gotten to me like this one does. No one's ever wiggled beneath my guard to make me long for things that aren't even real.

Usually I push aside these realizations, determined to keep her at a distance, however I can.

Tonight—just for tonight—I let her in.

I let her in the way she let me in, telling me every heartbreaking detail of her early life. I want to tell her that it's made her strong. That every hardship she's endured has made her remarkable.

But I don't have the words, and I'm not sure she'd be ready to hear them even if I did.

Instead, I show her. I show her with kisses, first on her sassy mouth, then along the sensitive column of her throat.

I tell her with my hand drifting over her side, her hip, her thighs, until we're both panting for more. More touching, more contact, more everything.

I slip a hand beneath her sweater to where her skin is hot and just the slightest bit damp. I unhook her bra, then slide my hand upward, palming her breast, heavy and perfect in my hand.

She groans, twisting her wrists to be released. I relent, only because I need her naked and writhing beneath me.

I peel her sweater over her head, both my hands cupping her breasts before the garment even hits the floor.

She says my name on a sigh, almost like a prayer instead of the usual curse. I close my eyes, trying to shut out the importance of the moment, then realizing I don't want to.

I open them, looking into her face as I use my fingers to tease her nipples, holding her gaze as I lower my mouth to her.

I know this woman's body better than I've known anyone else's, and I know that for all her strong feistiness, her breasts are sensitive. I keep my touch light and teasing, my kisses soft and fleeting.

When I finally wrap my mouth around a nipple, sucking with gentle pressure, she arches into me, her hands holding my head close.

I've never been so damn hard, and my need to drive into her is strong.

Instead, I ease my hand beneath the elastic of her yoga pants, stroking her lightly over the soft fabric of her underwear until wetness greets my fingers.

We both moan the moment my fingers slip beneath the fabric, touching her for real. She's wet and more than ready for me, but again I restrain myself from ripping off the rest of our clothes and burying myself deep. I want to be careful with her, want to prolong the moment.

I stroke two fingers over her, pressing and circling, teasing, until her panting breaths are punctuated with pleas. I ease a finger inside her, my thumb circling.

The moment before she comes, she stiffens slightly, and I move up, capturing her mouth and every cry as she tenses around my fingers, bucking beneath my hand.

I know then that I'm totally lost to this woman, because bringing her release feels damn near better than anything I've experienced in the past.

The moment doesn't last long as a peak sexual experience, though. The minutes that follow far surpass it.

She pushes me to my back, her hands drifting over me, getting rid of my clothes, kicking off the rest of hers until we're both naked and shaking with need.

My hands find her hips, urging her forward, over me, but she wiggles away, bending and wrapping her lips around me. I fall back on the pillow with a groan, my hand reaching out, skimming over her back, over her perfect ass, then up again, fingers tangling in her hair.

I let her work her magic as long as I can stand it, which I'm embarrassed to say isn't very long.

My hips arch, and I pull her back with a gasp. I need her, but not like this. I need . . . "Inside," I manage.

Sabrina doesn't hesitate. She digs around in my wallet for a condom and rolls it on. She moves over me, pausing for a heartbeat, then lowering, sinking onto me. Clenching around me.

We freeze as our eyes lock, acknowledging the moment. The importance of it.

Then my hands find her hips, and we begin to move. She sets the rhythm, sultry and languid, and I cooperate. Up until a point.

I lift, moving deeper, urging her on. *More.*

She complies, her hips circling faster. Her head dips back, her hair wild down her back, her breasts on display in all their perfection.

I'm gone. She destroys me. With my last ounce of self-control, I press my thumb to her center, ensuring that she falls with me when I go over the edge.

We don't just fall. We fly.

Until we crash.

She collapses forward, and I pull her to me, rolling us to our sides, our bodies still joined, our beating hearts pressed together in a thundering rhythm.

When I catch my breath, I press a kiss to her forehead, and her hand slides over my waist, drifting over my back in an idle caress.

After a few more moments of silence, I feel her smile against my chest. "I'm not doing very well with my no-hookup rule, huh?"

I smile and smooth back her hair, pulling away slightly so I can see her face. "You didn't hear me complaining. Besides, I figure we're smart enough to get away with it."

"Get away with what?" she asks, tracing a nail down the center of my chest.

"Sex without the other stuff." *Love.*

"Ah," she says lightly, and I know she heard my silent addition.

We say nothing more as we drift into a sated sleep, and it's not until I wake much later that I realize she didn't confirm my sex-without-love assessment.

For the life of me, I don't know if I'm relieved or disappointed.

28

Sabrina

Sunday Night, October 8

"For the tenth time, you don't have to escort me up here."

"You know, that'd be a lot more convincing if you had a purse dog and were a light packer," Matt says as he detangles Juno's leash from my roller bag again. "As I see it, you have a huge dog who can't walk five steps without getting tangled up in a suitcase packed for a European relocation instead of a weekend getaway."

"You can just say you're mad that I made you go to that farmer's market today," I say, sniffing the enormous bouquet I have cradled in one arm while being careful not to drop the large white pumpkin in the other.

"I'm not mad. But I still maintain that you over packed. And that pumpkins are supposed to be orange."

"White pumpkins are very in right now," I say, setting said white pumpkin on the floor at my feet so I can pull out my keys.

Matt unclips Juno's leash from her collar, so she's the first one into the apartment. Matt and I follow, and though I'll never admit it out loud . . . it *is* a lot of stuff.

I'm not usually one for farmer's markets. Give me delivery or couture any day. But today, when Matt and I took Juno on a walk, we stumbled across one, and somehow I let myself get sucked into the charm of it.

I've been sucked into the charm of the entire weekend.

And much as I know it was probably a mistake, I can't bring myself to regret a single moment. Not the long lingering meals, the champagne-fueled brunches, the sex, none of it.

Spilling my guts on Friday night had been scary, but it had also done something wonderful for the rest of the weekend.

See: farmers market.

Also . . .

I give Matt a coy glance, waiting to see if he'll bring it up first.

He catches my eye and grins as he refills Juno's water dish. "I'm not asking for it."

"But you know you want to."

"Oh, I want to," he agrees, setting the dish in front of my panting dog. "But I want to win more."

I purse my lips. I like winning, too. But I also like my cell phone. The worst part is, it was my own idea.

On Friday night as we waited for the steaks to finish grilling, I noticed both Matt and I checking our iPhones, I suspect more out of habit than anything else. I issued a challenge: Who could go the longest without it? We turned them off then and there and traded, so neither would be tempted to sneak a look while the other was in a different room.

It was weird, but also surprisingly freeing.

I can't remember the last time I've simply let myself be present in a moment, any moment. There's something entirely too vulnerable about being alone with your thoughts, with no Facebook distraction, no incoming email, no matter how inconsequential.

There's something even more vulnerable about being alone with your thoughts . . . and your worst enemy.

Except he's not.

And if I'm honest, he hasn't been for a long time.

Hell, to be completely honest, I don't know that he was ever my worst enemy, so much as my biggest threat. The person who I sensed, even from the very beginning, could destroy me.

What I *didn't* see until recently was how the person with the power to destroy you can also be the one to lift you up. The one who can make you live like you've never lived before. The one who shines light into dark, infiltrates color into blandness.

The person who can take someone who's perfectly content and make her . . . happy.

The person who can make *me* happy.

Which, I'm sad to say, I didn't even know was possible. I've gotten so damn used to thinking anything better than hungry and angry was the good life.

Ian's always made me feel safe, in a big-brother kind of way. I thought that was as good as it gets. These past couple of weeks with Matt have changed that. Hell, these past four years with him have changed it. The way he makes me feel has always made me want to run.

But not anymore. Now I want to . . . *stay.*

I just wish I knew what comes next. I've never done this before. I've never fallen for someone, much less someone who's every bit as relationship averse as I am.

Matt, oblivious to my thoughts, pulls my cell phone out of his back pocket and gives it an enticing waggle. "Hmm?"

I bite my lip. I really do want that cell phone. I take his phone out of my bag and hold it up. "Call it a draw?"

"Done," he says in relief.

We swap phones, and I pour us each a sparkling water as I wait for my iPhone to start back up again after being powered off.

"So, here's a question," Matt says, accepting the glass I hold out. "You make a decent living, and I've seen firsthand you're damn good at your job. But what does your work look like on an average day?"

"Depends on whether or not I'm on an active project. When I sign a contract, that person's my priority. But assuming they don't need me 24-7, I generally keep my ear to the ground, stay in touch with my contacts. Coffee dates, lunch dates, whatever. As I approach the end of a project, I'll start figuring out what's next."

"How do you bring in new business?" he asks curiously.

I give a sly smile. "I don't. It finds me. Truth be told, I have more requests than I can possibly take on. I get to pick and choose what I work on."

He smiles. "Lucky for me I caught you at a slow time, then."

I take another sip of my drink and look away, not quite ready to tell him that there's no such thing as a slow time for me. That when he'd asked for my help, I had nearly a dozen other opportunities, some that would have gladly paid triple what he's paying for my assistance.

Instead, I'd taken on Matt's job. Not because the money was the best, not even because his case was the most interesting. But because it was *Matt.*

And he'd needed me.

Do I regret it? No.

I just wish I could do it over again, this time not falling in love with the man. But maybe that's not possible. Maybe I've been headed down this path with him since that very first night.

It doesn't matter, I suppose. How I got here isn't important. What *does* matter is that the feeling isn't going away anytime soon, and I need to decide what the heck I plan to do about it.

It's rare that I don't feel completely in control, and I don't like it. At all.

"So what is next?" Matt asks, leaning on my counter. I see that his phone's already rebooted, but his attention's still on me. As though what I have to say is important.

"Well, the gala's more than a week away, so officially, I'm still on your payroll," I say.

"And after the gala?"

"I've got my pick." I twist the glass on the counter. "I've got an invitation to spend a couple weeks playing companion to a ridiculously wealthy eighty-year-old in Florence whose son thinks she's got a bad habit of getting engaged to fortune hunters. There's a lotto winner from Jersey who wants me to wrangle an invitation for his daughter to meet a prince. Any prince. A midtown lawyer wants me to play flavor of the week to make an ex-girlfriend jealous."

"No," Matt says. "Not that last one."

I smile at the note of jealousy in his voice. "Does it make a difference if the lawyer's a woman?"

He opens his mouth but hesitates. Then shakes his head. "I still vote no. Though I realize I don't have any claim on your time past the gala."

You could. All you'd have to do is ask.

But I don't have the guts to tell him, and he doesn't have the guts to ask.

Or worse, maybe he doesn't even want to.

I bite my lip, wondering if I should remind him of Jarod Lanham's interest in my services. I decide against it. If Jarod *does* decide to hire me, and if I decide to take him on as a client, he deserves the same privacy I give all my clients.

Matt picks up his cell phone, and I do the same. There are a couple dozen new emails. That's expected.

There are also several voice mails and text messages. That's not expected. My email address is on my business card—plenty of people have it. My phone number? Only a select few in my inner circle have it. Ian. Kate and Lara.

All three of them have texted me. Multiple times.

Ian: Call me.

Lara: Thank God you're not the freak-out type. Right? You're not freaking, are you? Let me know.

Neither of theirs tells me what's going on. Kate's is more helpful.

Kate: OMG. What? Read this. Then explain.

A link to a gossip site accompanies her text, and, when I click on it, the headline tells me everything I need to know.

WALL STREET'S MOST NOTORIOUS PLAYBOY PUTS A RING ON IT . . .

The accompanying picture is Matt and me at dinner last night, sharing a bottle of wine and looking, well . . . intimate. Though how the hell someone looked at this and figured *engaged* is beyond me.

A quick skim of the article, and I have my answer. It's nothing but a case of good old-fashioned bullshit. A "source close to the couple" claimed that I'd been dress shopping. *False.*

That we'd been considering Saint John's as the site of the ceremony. *False.*

That we'd already booked tickets to New Zealand for our honeymoon. *False.*

That Matt had been seen in Tiffany & Co., looking at engagement rings. *Super false.*

I let out a little laugh at the audaciousness of it all. It never ceases to amaze me how much of this stuff is made up. Granted, this time, it works in our favor, but it's still worthy of an eye roll.

I look up at Matt and can tell from his scowl, he's gotten similar messages.

I lean forward with a teasing smile. "So. What kind of ring did you get me? I'm sort of partial to the traditional Tiffany cut, but as long as it's big and shiny . . ."

I break off when he lifts his head and meets my eyes. He doesn't look amused or even exasperated.

He looks . . .

Well, shoot. I can't tell.

"Hey," I say softly, reaching across the counter to touch his hand. "It's just a crap tabloid thing. People will forget about it."

He nods but doesn't say anything.

I smile a little wider, determined to erase the sudden awkwardness that's descended. And more important, to eradicate the longing in my heart. The desire for it to be real. "Looks like we did our job a little too well, right? I mean, I knew I was good, but even I didn't know—"

"What if we did it?" he interrupts.

I frown in confusion. "Did what?"

"Got married."

My mouth drops open, even as my stomach flips. "That's taking the charade a bit far, don't you think?"

His jaw tenses, and he looks down at the floor before looking up once more. "What if it wasn't a charade?"

I put a hand to my still-fluttering stomach. "Matt. You don't want to get married."

"Not in the traditional sense, no," he says. "But I wouldn't mind trying it your way."

"My way?"

"You know. Sex. Companionship. None of the emotional, messy stuff."

I can't breathe. Somehow this moment feels like my ultimate fantasy and my worst nightmare, all rolled into one confusing, heartbreaking moment. Because now I know I want so much more.

"I can't," I whisper.

"Why not?" he says, his voice urgent as he steps closer. "I've enjoyed these past few weeks, and I know you have, too. You said yourself, you want someone to come home to at the end of the night, and . . .

hell, why can't that someone be me? We know we'd fight, but we also know the make-up sex would be outstanding. We respect each other, and neither of us would have to pretend that we're the next great love story—"

"I *can't,*" I repeat, more desperately this time.

Matt frowns in concern at my tone, reaching out a hand toward me. "It's okay; I know it's sudden. You need time to think, and—"

"No." I shake my head and close my eyes. "I mean, yes, it is sudden, but that's not why I'm saying no."

When I open my eyes again, his expression is shuttered and unreadable. "Why are you saying no?"

I take a deep breath. "Because you don't love me."

Matt's eyes widen slightly in shock. "Well . . . no. I mean . . . I don't really do that. But neither do you."

I bite my bottom lip so hard my eyes water. Actually, no. My eyes are watering for another reason entirely. This *hurts.*

"Sabrina." His tone is sharp. "You don't love me. Do you?"

I take a deep breath as I realize I owe it to him—and to myself—to be completely honest.

Forcing a smile, I lift my shoulders and let them fall. "Apparently, I do. And knowing what that feels like now, I don't think I can do marriage the companionship-only way I always imagined. I want . . . more. I want a real marriage. And I don't think I can settle for less."

29

Matt

Sunday Night, October 8

Sabrina's statement lingers in the air like the aftermath of an explosion, my shock rendering me speechless.

When I finally do manage words, they're hardly eloquent. *"What?"*

She flinches. "I know. I was surprised, too."

I don't move; I can only stare. "Sabrina, I thought—"

"It's not like I'm joining a cult, Cannon," she says, some of her usual sass returning.

"Might as well be." The words are cold and callous, and I don't mean them to be, not really. But to say she's caught me off guard here is an understatement. I can barely think clearly, much less speak eloquently.

Her blue eyes seem to blaze at me as she comes closer. "You're terrified."

Damn straight.

"I'm confused. Just a few days ago, we were on the same page. You yourself said you wanted to avoid the emotional, messy stuff."

"I know I did! And it's precisely because of moments like this," she says, sounding slightly frustrated. "Because this"—she gestures between us—"sucks."

"Exactly," I say, reaching out and grasping her shoulders. "So let it pass. It's just the proximity messing with your head. We can go back to the way we were, just friends who enjoy each other's company. Or we can go back to fighting."

Just don't leave me. Don't walk away.

"Look, Matt." She lifts her shoulders and eases away. "I'm not asking anything of you. I know I changed it up. You don't feel the same, and that's . . . f-fine."

She stutters over the word as though it pains her, then takes a deep breath and continues.

"I get it. I'm not exactly thrilled, either, but my feelings are there, and they're complicated, and they're not going away anytime soon. You don't want a wife who loves you, and I don't want a husband who doesn't love me. Where does that leave us?"

I close my eyes and try to sort out the mess of thoughts going through my head. "I don't know."

"Well I do," she says matter-of-factly, as though she didn't just drop the L-word up in here and destroy every good thing we had going on. "We need some space."

"I don't want some damned space!" I shout, opening my eyes again. "I want . . . I want . . ."

"What?" she says.

You.

I try to tell her out loud, but the words don't come. It's as though they're buried deep, lodged in my throat.

"I want things back the way they were," I say instead, hating the pleading note in my voice but unable to hold it back.

She says nothing.

I'm losing her. I know I'm losing her, and yet the only way of keeping her is to take that idiotic plunge, to go over the edge with her, and risk everything.

I won't do it. She matters too much.

"Sabrina," I say quietly, closing the distance between us. "You know I care about you . . ."

Her face twists. "Don't. Please don't do that."

I clench my fists in impatience. "Don't what, speak the truth?"

"Not if the truth involves some sort of placating *but*. You care about me, *but*. You want to keep sleeping with me, *but*. That's what I'm trying to tell you. I want what we have *without* the buts. I want what Ian and Lara have. What I suspect The Sams have. I want someone to be with me not just because it's convenient and we're well suited but because he can't stand the thought of not being with me."

I swallow, thinking of my parents. Thinking of how they made all those promises to each other, how they were supposedly once like Ian and Lara, but none of it lasted.

I think of how they are now. Indifferent to each other.

I won't do that to Sabrina. I won't do that to *us*.

But neither can I bear to see her unhappy. If this is what she needs . . .

I reach out and gently cup her face, my thumbs drifting over her cheeks. "I'm sorry I can't give you what you want," I say quietly. "But if you want to chase the fairy-tale ending, I won't stand in your way."

Her face crumples for a moment, but she recovers almost immediately, giving a quick nod. "Thank you. I still need some space, though, Matt. I can't fall in love with someone else as long as I'm in love with you."

I feel her words like a knife in my chest.

But I nod, knowing what she means. No more casual sex when it suits us. No more verbal foreplay disguised as arguments. And for me, no fellow realist—no more safety in Sabrina's shared knowledge that love destroys relationships, not fosters it.

"Still friends?" she says, sounding more vulnerable than I've ever heard her.

My gut clenches at the word, somehow both vitally important and not nearly enough. "Of course," I whisper, setting my forehead to hers. "Of course."

Our arms slowly find their way around each other, and there's a desperation to the goodbye hug—not forever, not for good, but goodbye to the way we were. The way we've become.

I press a lingering kiss to her temple. "Be happy."

I hear her swallow, then she nods.

I pull back, intending to give her my standard cocky smile, but I can't summon it forth. Not when I see the unshed tears in her eyes.

Her hands drop from my waist, and I release her with a backward step.

I walk to her front door, knowing she won't stop me. She wants love. I want her to have it.

And I wish like hell I had it in me to give it.

30

Sabrina

Monday Lunch, October 16

"So, are we going to talk about it, or are you going to keep pretending everything's cool?"

I look at Ian over my Diet Coke. "You mandated this meeting. You have something say, say it."

It's Monday afternoon, a little more than a week since Matt basically proposed marriage.

Sans love.

I'm trying really hard not to think about it. Or him.

But Ian's making it difficult. Because as much as I know that he's my best friend and loves me like a sister, he *also* loves Matt like a brother.

It's hard to share a meal with *this* man without thinking of *the* man.

Ian pushes aside his plate and, crossing both arms on the table, studies me with his piercing blue eyes. I can't help but compare them to another pair of blue eyes. Ian's are ice-blue, slightly almond-shaped. Matt's eyes are dark blue, the ocean on a sunny day, wide and bright and . . .

I suck in a sharp intake of breath as the pain hits. Again. I know it'll pass. Eventually.

But damn, this sucks.

Damn, it had hurt to stand there and put my heart out there, knowing he didn't feel the same, and have him all but shake my hand and wish me well.

I take a bite of my tuna Nicoise salad and pretend not to notice Ian's scrutiny.

"He's irritable," Ian announces.

I nip a green bean cleanly with my front teeth. "Who?"

My best friend's look is withering. "Really?"

Fine. I sigh and set aside my fork. "I'm sorry Cannon's acting like a juvenile, but it's really not my problem. I sent him an email letting him know that I'd be happy to continue our working relationship through the end of the contract despite our personal entanglements. He's yet to take me up on the offer."

"An email," Ian repeats. "You two make love and war like both are going out of style for the better part of the past God knows how many years, and you sit there and tell me you sent him an email?"

"What do you want me to do here, Ian? What do you want me to say?"

"I want you to tell me what happened."

I sip my soda. "Ask him."

"I *did* ask him. Kennedy asked him. Kate asked him. Half the office thinks he received a six-months-to-live sentence from his doctor, that's how unhappy he's been."

"And that's my fault because . . . ?"

Ian throws up his hands in frustration. "I swear, I don't know why I try to talk to either of you."

"Well, I just don't see why I'm supposed to shoulder the blame for Matt's irritability. Maybe it's work related. Has he heard anything on the Jarod front?"

I keep my voice casual, careful not to betray the real reason I agreed to meet Ian for lunch. It's not that I don't enjoy my best friend, but as I said, seeing Ian makes me think of Matt, and, well, lately . . . that's painful as all get out.

Ian's eyebrows lift at my question. "*Jarod?* You and the world's most famous billionaire are on a first-name basis?"

I fiddle with my fork, knowing that I'm going to have to rip this Band-Aid off sometime. Might as well be now.

"He's been in touch."

Okay, so I chickened out a little bit. That's the truth but not the *whole* truth. We'll get to that part later.

Ian reaches across the table and snags an olive from my plate. "You and Lanham have been in touch . . . how?"

"Mr. Lanham got my email and reached out."

Ian sits back in his chair. "Ten seconds ago, he was 'Jarod.' You can't go all formal on me now."

"I can do whatever I want."

"Cut the bullshit, Sabrina. You're the most direct person I know, so this whole cagey thing isn't suiting you."

I swallow, a little stung by the rebuke, even though I know it was well deserved. "Jarod wants to hire me," I say, sipping my soda.

"For what?"

"That's between him and me."

"Sabrina—"

I hold up a hand. "No, I draw the line there. I don't share my clients' requests with anyone, even you. You'd expect the same privacy if you hired me."

"I *have* hired you," he points out. "You got me the best lawyer in the city when I needed one."

"I did that because you're my best friend," I say, waving my hand. "The point is, when someone asks for my help, I'm a vault."

"But the whole group knows about your ruse with Cannon."

"Because it was half your idea," I point out. "Had Matt come to me for help on his own and asked me to keep it between us, I wouldn't have told a soul."

"Not even me?" Ian gives his best smile.

"Not even you, you pain in the ass."

"You and your pesky professional ethics," he says, shaking his head. "Okay, fine, don't tell me what Lanham wants. Can you at least tell me what happened between you and Matt? As a friend?"

I hesitate, then realize that though I don't particularly want to talk about it, maybe I need to. Goodness knows trying to bury it deep and pretend it doesn't exist hasn't been serving me well for the past week. I'm not sleeping, I'm barely eating . . .

I take a deep breath and look up. "It would seem I fell in love with the idiot."

I'm prepared for Ian's shock, but I see none. Instead he gives me a sympathetic smile. "Yeah. I figured."

"Did you?" I murmur. "Might have been nice if you would've mentioned it. To me."

"Yeah, I can just imagine how well that conversation would have gone."

I lift my elbows to the table and drop my head tiredly into my hands. "How did this happen? *Why* did this happen?"

Ian smiles slightly. "Does he know how you feel?"

I nod once, not particularly wanting to relive the moment in which I admitted my feelings and Matt did . . . nothing.

"And?"

I lift my head, not quite able to tell him about Matt's proposal, but I say enough to give him the gist. "He suggested. . . sex. Companionship . . ."

Everything I *thought* I wanted. Everything that just until a week or so ago I would've probably been perfectly satisfied with. Someone to take the dog out when it rains, someone to laugh with. Heck, even someone to argue with, which I know sounds nuts, but even at our worst moments, fighting with Matt made me feel alive.

I wish I didn't want more. I wish I didn't want it all—the life partner *and* the fairy tale.

I meet Ian's gaze miserably. "I don't just want someone to be with. I want someone to love me."

He reaches across the table and gives my arm a brotherly squeeze. "Of course you do. You deserve that, Sabrina."

I smile faintly. "Try telling Matt that."

"I shouldn't have to," he mutters. Ian's gaze turns considering. "You're sure he doesn't feel the same way? Because the way he's been acting—"

"Ian, you weren't there. You didn't see his face. Whatever I feel for him . . . it's not mutual. Or if it is, it's not strong enough on his side for him to be brave enough to act on it."

Ian's head drops in defeat. "For someone so smart, he's such a fucking idiot."

I pick up my Diet Coke and chew my straw in agitation, a habit I thought I'd kicked by the time I was twelve. "Agreed."

"So what happens now?"

I shrug. "Eventually I'll get over my feelings for him, and he and I can go back to the way we were."

"The whole enemies-with-benefits thing?" Ian asks with a wince.

"No, not that." I continue to chew my straw. "I think . . . I think I want to date. I want to find someone for *real.* Much as this whole love thing hurts like hell, I don't know that I want to settle for anything less."

"You shouldn't," Ian says firmly. "But you know you can't go treating this like a project. You can't just decide to fall in love with someone. Especially not when you're in love with someone else."

"I know," I say with a sigh. "It's annoying, but I know. But I can start putting myself out there, right?"

"Sure," he says slowly. "After a time. When you're ready."

I say nothing, and he gives me a knowing look.

"Sabrina, what are you not telling me?"

I take a deep breath, already having a good sense of just how well my bombshell is going to go over. "Jarod Lanham is going to give Matt his business," I say.

"*What?* He told you that?"

"Yes. He'll give Matt his business . . . *if* I go to the Wolfe Gala with him."

"Seriously?" Ian looks shocked and confused, and I don't blame him. The situation is . . . odd.

"I met with Jarod a couple days ago, regarding a potential business venture," I say. "He congratulated me on my 'engagement,' and I told him that the rumors weren't based on fact."

"Sabrina—"

"I didn't tell him that the thing with Matt and me was a ruse," I say, holding up a hand to stop his objections. "I just clarified that the engagement wasn't true."

"Then why would he ask you to the gala, if he thinks you and Matt are still an item? Seems like the ultimate dick move to me."

It does, sort of. To be honest, I don't have a clue what Jarod's angle is. This whole thing with Matt's apparently thrown me off my game, because instead of being able to assess someone's motives in an instant, I'd shared an entire meal with Jarod, and I don't have a clue where his head's at.

"Surely you're not thinking about agreeing—" Ian says.

"Hear me out," I interrupt. "This thing with Matt and me isn't real. He hired me to pretend to be in a relationship with him to clean up his reputation *so that he can get clients like Jarod Lanham*. I honestly don't think Matt will care how it happens, so long as it happens. Lanham's always been the goal."

"So you're going to do it?"

"I don't know yet. It really should be Matt's decision," I say. "We signed a contract that I'd accompany him to any events, specifically the gala. But I can't imagine he wouldn't prefer to have Jarod as a client."

"And how will you feel about that?"

"Does it matter?"

"It does to me."

I take a deep breath and consider.

Honestly? I'm tired of feeling. I wouldn't mind being numb, just for a little while. I meant what I said to Ian about wanting to hold out for the fairy-tale ending, but . . . not just yet. I need time to come to grips with my feelings for Matt and embrace them, agony and all.

But . . . I'd be lying if I said Jarod's interest hasn't been a balm to my ego. It gives me hope to know that just because I'm alone *now*, just because my heart hurts now, it doesn't mean I'll have to be alone *forever*.

I'll go to the gala with Matt if that's what he wants, but I can't say that I'd look forward to it. Not with this weird unrequited-love thing I have going on now. I don't know that I'd particularly enjoy going with Jarod, either, but it would hurt less.

"I just want Matt to be happy," I say quietly. "His career's everything to him, and landing a client like Jarod would go a long way to restoring other clients' faith in him."

"Have you talked to him about it yet?"

I shake my head. "I was going to swing by the Wolfe offices later this afternoon. Kate says he's got some free time."

"Let me do it," Ian says.

I blink in surprise. "Why?"

"It's a guy thing."

"Well, for me it's a professional thing," I counter. "I can't let my client's coworker deliver this kind of news."

"You're not. You're letting your best friend talk to his best friend about a sticky situation."

"But—"

"Sabrina." He touches my arm again. "Trust me on this."

I open my mouth to tell him no—to tell him that best friend or not, I handle my own problems. Always have, always will.

But then . . . *have* I handled my own problems? Because over the past month I seem to have gotten myself into trouble, not out of it.

Surely Ian can't do any worse than I've done for myself.

"Fine," I say with a sigh. "Talk to him."

31

Matt

Tuesday Morning, October 17

"What the *fuck*? Tell me you're joking."

Ian takes a sip of his coffee. "Nope."

"Sabrina wants to go to the gala with Lanham?"

"Not what I said. I said *he* wants to go with *her*."

I suddenly have a whole new respect for the simplicity of cavemen's thoughts, because right now, I'd love nothing better than a big stick and a cliff, just Lanham and me fighting to the death, with him going over the edge.

"This is bullshit," I mutter.

"Did you miss the part where you get to manage all of Lanham's money?" Kennedy says from where he leans against the wall on the far side of my office.

"Yeah, but the asshole is using Sabrina as leverage. How am I the only one outraged by this?"

"Because," Kate says, coming through my open office door and unabashedly entering the conversation, "what he's doing is not that different from what you did to her."

I glare at her. "It's entirely different. And how do you know about this?"

Kate shuts the door and shakes her head, coming to sit across from me, beside Ian. "Sabrina told me. And it *isn't* different. You used her to get him. He used you to get her. You and Jarod want different things, but you still used someone else to get it."

"The parallels really are remarkable," Kennedy muses.

"Shut up," I growl at him. "How are all three of you sitting there like this is fine? Like it's no big deal that the woman I . . ."

"Yes?" Kate asks, sitting back and crossing her legs. "I'm *dying* to know how you're going to finish that sentence."

"I wouldn't mind hearing the answer to that one myself," Ian says. His tone is mild, but there's a note of warning there.

I lock eyes with him. "You've talked to her."

"Yes. We had lunch yesterday. That's when she told me about the Lanham deal."

"Fuck Lanham," I say, leaning forward. "How is she?"

There's a moment of silence in my office. Finally, Kennedy breaks it. "Did you just say, 'Fuck Lanham'? As in, the unicorn you've been chasing your entire career?"

I ignore this, never looking away from Ian. "How is she?"

"She's like you'd expect," Ian says.

"What the hell does that mean?" My desperation is coming out in my voice, but I don't care.

I *am* desperate.

It's been more than a week since I've seen her. Talked to her. Held her. And the absence of her feels like a gaping hole in my chest.

Her email that she was still available "per our contract" had only made matters worse, shining light on the fact that I don't want her that way. I don't want her to spend time with me because it's in the contract, because I'm paying her. I don't want her to pretend to be in love with me for the sake of my bosses and my damn reputation.

I want . . .

I want her to love me for real.

She does, you idiot. You were just too chickenshit to do anything about it.

Kate leans toward Ian without looking away from me. "Is he having a moment right now?" She says it in a whisper, but it's clearly meant for my ears.

I'm not having a moment. I've been having a *week.*

Or rather, a lifetime's realization in a week, without a damn clue of what happens next. What do I do? How do I get her back? How do I trust that I have what it takes?

"Are your parents happy?" I ask Kate.

She blinks in surprise. "My parents?"

"I've met them once. They seemed happy."

"Sure, they're happy. Married thirty-two years next month, and they still act like they're on their honeymoon."

Thirty-two years of happiness.

I shift my gaze to Kennedy. "What about your parents? Happy?"

He gives me a questioning look but nods. "Yeah, they're happy."

I glance at Ian, who shrugs. "Everyone knows my parents aren't in the picture, and my foster father's longest relationship is with the Phillies. But if you're after what I think you're after—reassurance that a man and a woman can be happy together long-term—I can assure you that it's absolutely possible for two people who love each other to make it work. It may not be easy. It's terrifying as shit. But it's possible."

Kate pats Ian's knee affectionately. "I can't say I ever imagined the day when you'd play the role of love coach, but it's an adorable look on you."

If I didn't know better, I'd swear Ian is blushing just a little, but given my own predicament at the moment, I'm hardly one to give him shit.

"You know what I mean," Ian grumbles. "I'm just saying Cannon should get over whatever moronic hang-ups he has about relationships."

"What are your hang-ups?" Kennedy asks. "Just good old-fashioned male commitment phobia?"

"Something like that."

My friends' silence tells me my answer isn't good enough.

I sigh. "Fine. My parents' relationship is completely fucked up. It'd be one thing if they just got divorced, you know? Allowed each other to move on? Instead they just sort of accepted that their bullshit arrangement was as good as it gets."

"Which led you to believe that that would be as good as it ever got for *you*?" Kate asks, sounding slightly disappointed in me.

I don't bother to defend myself, because I'm disappointed, too. I've been an idiot and a coward, too foolish to see that my feelings for Sabrina aren't terrifying because they're wrong—they're terrifying because they're right.

She's right. For me.

"What if I said no?" I ask. "What if I held her to the contract, told her not to go to the gala with Lanham?"

"You'd lose him as a client, but I don't think that's what you're really asking," Ian says.

"No, it's not. I want to know if I still have a chance with her. To fix this."

"You're not going to find out by forcing her into anything with that damn contract," Kennedy says.

Kate points to Kennedy without looking at him. "For once, the cyborg gets it right. You walked away when she was at her most vulnerable. You don't get her back by making her go to the gala with you."

"Well, I can't let her go with some other guy."

"Actually, that's exactly what you do," Ian says.

I'm already shaking my head. "If he takes Sabrina to the gala, I get his business, and she'll think I want to get my cake and eat it, too, or whatever the hell that phrase is."

"Where did that phrase come from?" Kennedy muses. "Marie Antoinette?"

"No, that's *let them eat cake*," Kate says. "I think *have your cake and eat it, too* is in reference—"

"Guys," I interrupt. "A little help here?"

"Okay, okay, sorry," Kate says. "I think I get where Ian's going with this. You let Sabrina go to the gala with the hot billionaire . . ."

I wince. The mental picture of Sabrina on another guy's arm makes me physically ill.

"*And* you turn down Lanham's business," Ian finishes.

I suck in a breath. I knew, on some level, where they were going with this, what has to be done. But I'm not going to say the prospect of losing out on Jarod Lanham doesn't sting.

It's just that the thought of losing Sabrina hurts more. *A lot* more.

"The Sams won't like it," I say.

"Nope," Kennedy confirms. "They'll be pissed."

"Do you care?" Ian asks.

I meet his eyes. "I care. I just care about her more."

"Do you love her?" Kate asks, going for broke.

Love.

It's a word I've never really given much thought to, partially because I didn't think it was for me. But mostly because . . .

I've been terrified. Still am, to be honest. But if anyone's worth it, *she* is.

Instead of answering Kate's question, I turn my attention to the guys. "Remember a few weeks back when we were taking about . . . What did you call it? The Cinderella complex?"

"The what now?" Kate asks.

"You know . . . when a woman puts on a fancy dress, goes to a dance, becomes determined to find her Prince Charming."

She rolls her eyes. "Uh-huh. That's us women, all right. It's a wonder we can even manage to fit in the hunt for the prince, what with all the powdering of our noses."

"Okay, but we picked Sabrina for your plan because we knew she'd be immune to the Cinderella complex," Ian says, ignoring Kate.

"Which is why I need your help," I say, trying to maintain my patience for what feels like the most important undertaking of my life. "I need to figure out how to make Sabrina *un*-immune."

"Let me get this straight," Kennedy says. "Instead of *avoiding* the Cinderella complex, you want to activate it? At the cost of your dream client and potentially the cost of your job?"

I nod. "You once told me that Lanham was the thing I wanted more than anything. You were wrong."

"You want Sabrina," Ian says. "But for how long?"

"I want Sabrina . . . forever. For always."

The guys look a bit shocked, but Kate merely smiles in triumph. "I knew it. You love her."

I brace for the stab of panic, and I'm freaked out, all right, but not in the way I expected to be.

I'm not in panic over my love for her. On the contrary, loving Sabrina might just be the most sane, smartest thing I've ever done.

I love her. I love her more than anything.

My panic? Fear that I might be too late—that she might no longer love *me*.

32

Sabrina

Saturday Evening, October 21

Dressing up's a regular part of my job—jeans are a luxury, sweatpants almost unheard of.

Black-tie, however, is a whole other ball game and one I secretly enjoy.

The Wolfe Gala is one of maybe a half dozen annual events I attend, and I've got a handful of dresses that meet the black-tie criteria. A sleek, classic black. A low-cut red ball gown when I need to own the room. A demure light-purple dress with lace overlay to play up the ingénue effect. A borderline dowdy emerald-green dress for when I need to fly under the radar.

When I thought I'd be attending with Matt, none of my usual dresses felt quite right. So before the weekend in the Hamptons, before everything *imploded*, I went out and splurged on something new.

I picked out a dress with zero agenda beyond my wanting to feel pretty. I settled on one that's strapless and fitted up top, with a flowing A-line skirt.

The cut is simple. The color is not.

The dress is several shades of shimmering, silvery blue that create an almost ombré effect. The saleswoman had compared it to a moonbeam, and as whimsical as I thought the comparison was at the time, she's exactly right.

I've let my hair down and styled it straighter than usual to mimic the sleek lines of the bodice, a small discreet set of diamond studs my only accessory.

The entire finished look is everything I hoped for.

All for the wrong man.

"More champagne?" Jarod says, touching a hand to my back and nodding at my nearly empty glass.

I smile. "Please."

He exchanges our glasses for new ones from a passing waiter, then hands me one. "I've been to my fair share of fancy parties, but I'll admit I'm impressed."

I take a sip of champagne and survey the room. The Wolfe Gala's been at the same museum on the West Side for the past couple of years, but they changed it up this year. It's at a stunning mansion on Park Avenue, one only recently converted to an event space, and I'd have to agree with Jarod's assessment.

The combination of bright-white walls, black marble floors, and chandeliers gives the room a timeless elegance, with the dark-red accents scattered around the room adding a bit of richness.

"I haven't seen your Boy Wonder around," Jarod says, scanning the crowd.

I take a sip of champagne to swallow back a retort that though Matt's brilliant, he's hardly a boy. He's not mine to defend.

He's not mine at all.

"I wasn't surprised to learn he agreed to my terms, but I'll confess I'm glad he did," Jarod says, his gaze returning to me, drifting briefly over my dress. "I appreciate your coming with me tonight. And if I haven't said it already, you look lovely."

I'm relieved that the compliment seems more matter-of-fact than anything, the way one might compliment a sibling or platonic friend. In this regard, Jarod's been a perfect gentleman all night.

I'm still not entirely sure what his agenda is, but I'm not even sure I care. Jarod Lanham is the least of my worries these days.

"How did Cannon handle the news?" Jarod asks, furthering my suspicion that his game has more to do with Matt than it does with me.

"You don't know?" I ask, tilting my head.

Jarod's tuxedoed shoulders shrug. "Honestly? I haven't heard from him. I wasn't even sure he got the news until you called to tell me you'd go with me tonight."

I carefully hide my puzzlement. Ian called me two nights ago to let me know he'd filled Matt in on Jarod's terms. Yesterday, I'd gotten a revised contract from Matt, terminating our agreement. There'd also been a check for the precise amount we'd agreed to.

Getting the contract and the money had been both gut-wrenching and relieving. It's the *relief* I've been clinging to. Relief that the sooner Matt and I end this thing, the sooner I can move on.

As for the check, I'd promptly given it to Ian as a donation for his charity for underprivileged high school students. They need it more than I do, and I didn't think I'd be able to stomach the thought of keeping a single penny from my time with Matt.

Our time together was worth a hell of a lot more to me, even if it ended badly.

A middle-aged couple I don't recognize stops to socialize with Jarod, and after he makes the introductions, I allow my mind to wander, studying Jarod as he talks, trying to figure him out.

He really is attractive, in a commanding-presence sort of way, and he wears a tux like he was born in one. He's also considerate, smart, and has a subtle, dry sense of humor.

The whole billionaire thing doesn't hurt, either.

And yet, no matter how hard I try, I can't see myself with him. I can't see myself with anyone except the one guy who's either too scared to take a risk or too disinterested to even *consider* it.

Still, knowing that, I can't help but scan the room for Matt. Even when we were at our most antagonistic, he'd always been a beacon for my attention, so though there are dozens of tuxedos in the room, I know almost immediately that he's not one of them.

Which is odd. Attendance at this thing is pretty much mandatory for all Wolfe employees.

I've already seen Lara and Ian, though every time I get a free moment, they're in conversation, or vice versa.

Jarod and I walked in with Kennedy and a tall, boring blonde whose name I've already forgotten.

And Kate's not here yet, courtesy of a last-minute zipper emergency on the dress she'd planned to wear. She asked if I could set her up with a tailor who could fix the zipper and the resulting tear, but I'd done her one better: I'd hooked her up with my girl at Saks, with instructions to send the bill to Kennedy, mostly because it amused me to do so.

Distractedly, I scan the room again. Still no Matt.

Maybe he's picking up his date.

My stomach lurches. Is he bringing a date? It didn't occur to me to ask Ian, and I wish I would have. Though I don't know that anything could prepare me for that. Just the thought of it makes me queasy.

Someone touches my arm, and I turn to see Lara, looking gorgeous in a long purple gown. She's forgone her usual glasses for the evening, but her hair's in a fancier version of her trademark ponytail, and the combination of elegant evening gown and sleek blonde ponytail is stunning.

"You look beautiful," I say, giving her a quick hug, and then spinning my finger so she'll show me the back of the dress. "Oh, well done," I say approvingly, taking in the low cut that leaves her back almost entirely bare. "Poor Ian must be dying."

"He's suggested no fewer than ten times that we make it an early night, but I've told him we have to stay at least as long as it took me to find the dress and get ready tonight, so he's stuck here for another hour or two."

"Well, well, don't you two clean up nice."

Lara and I turn, letting out twin gasps when we see Kate.

She's always pretty, but she seems somehow transformed tonight. Her usually straight, thick hair's been pulled into an elegant chignon to show off her petite features, and the dress is just about the sexiest thing I've ever seen.

The skirt's full and wide, which emphasizes her tiny waist, but it's really the bodice that steals the show. Tightly fitted to her tiny frame, the black satin alternating with black lace reveals glimpses of skin through the fabric. The effect is a combination of demure and seductive, and perfectly her.

"Thanks again for the assist," Kate tells me. "Your girl worked wonders."

"Let's not give her too much credit," I say. "She had an excellent muse to work with."

Kate blows me a kiss in acknowledgment. "So are we having fun?"

"We will be once Ian gets done making the rounds talking shop," Lara says, faking a small yawn. "I don't know how you guys get used to these fancy things."

"Truthfully, getting ready is the best part," Kate says.

"No, taking off the strapless bra at the end of the night is the best part," I correct.

"This backless dress didn't allow one of those, but not to worry, I have Spanx to punish me. Ian doesn't know what sweet, sexy surprise awaits." She surreptitiously snaps the waistband of said Spanx for emphasis.

I smile into my champagne, absolutely confident that Ian's not going to be the least bit deterred by Lara's shape wear. The woman could put on a dress made of dead leaves, and he'd still be crazy for her.

"Speaking of, anyone want to keep me company while I go to the ladies' room? The Spanx add five minutes to the peeing process, and I need someone to talk me through it over the stall wall."

"I'm game," Kate says, reaching out and taking my champagne, tossing it back. "It's not like I have a date."

"Yeah, why is that?" I ask. "Anybody looking like you shouldn't be alone."

Kate doesn't reply, but her eyes flick across the room. I follow her gaze, which is locked on Kennedy and his mannequin.

Oh, Kate.

I wish I could help with whatever it is she feels for Kennedy, but I don't know how much use I'd be. I can barely get a grasp on my own love life.

"Guys. My bladder?" Lara says, doing an awkward shuffle.

"Right. On it."

Yet another Wall Street bigwig has captured Jarod's attention, so I catch his eye and, after gesturing toward the girls, point in the direction of the ladies' room.

He gives a quick nod of acknowledgment.

Kate, Lara, and I are nearly to the hallway leading to the restrooms when someone steps directly into our path.

I blink a little in surprise, then smile when I realize it's a familiar face. "Dana, hi! I didn't realize you were coming here tonight."

"Yeah, well . . ." The tall, sharp-featured reporter gives a quick smile. "The news never sleeps."

Dana Keller's hair is red tonight, though I've also seen it black, blonde, silver, and just about every other color. The red suits her, though, as does her emerald gown.

"You're giving off a very Poison Ivy look tonight. I like it."

Generally speaking, I tolerate the media more than I actually enjoy them. They serve their purpose, and I know how to make them serve my purpose. But Dana and I go way back, and she's a journalist I actually like. She draws a hard line in the sand when it comes to reporting the facts and only the facts, so she's not one of my more easily manipulated contacts, but that only makes me respect her more.

I'm so surprised to see her at a fancy-pants event that I don't register the standard reporter notebook in her hand until it's too late.

She gives me a quick smile of apology, which makes my heart beat in overdrive panic. Dana Keller doesn't *do* apologies.

"Ms. Cross, is it true that you and Matt Cannon have been seeing each other?"

"What?" God, no, *please*. I am not strong enough to be bombarded with this right now.

"Dana—"

She interrupts, making no effort to keep her voice down, and several people look our way. "You've been seen on multiple occasions sharing meals, drinks, even shopping. Is it safe to assume those were dates?"

I quickly glance at Lara and Kate, but instead of looking horrified by Dana's ambush, they seem almost nervously excited. Traitors.

I try to move around the reporter, even as the crowd surrounding us grows more curious. "Dana. Please. Can we not do this right now?"

"There have even been reports that you're engaged. Can you confirm?"

"I can confirm that we're not," I snap. Then I frown as I realize she hasn't written down a single word. For that matter, Dana Keller would never conduct an interview without her ever-present recorder, which is nowhere in sight.

"And yet, several sources confirm that Mr. Cannon went ring shopping."

I refuse to show how much the questions sting. How much they remind me of what I won't have. "Your sources were wrong. Matt Cannon and I were seeing each other for a brief time, but the relationship has run its course. Now if you'll excuse me . . ."

I start to push around Dana, making a mental note to put her on my shit list until the end of time, when a male voice speaks out.

"Actually, the sources weren't wrong."

I whirl around, my heart pounding at the sound of Matt's voice, my breath catching at the sight of him. Why, even when I'm determined to hate him, does he have to look so perfect?

So perfect for *me*.

He looks amazing in his tuxedo, but that's not even the part that gets me. It's the familiar line of his jaw, the playful tilt of his smile, the warmth in his eyes . . .

I shake my head to snap out of my daze. "What are you talking about? What sources?"

"The sources that said I was ring shopping. Not wrong."

I'm not sure I've been speechless in my entire life, but I am now, stunned down to my very core.

Convinced I'm in a dream, I glance at Lara and Kate, who are smiling, albeit nervously. Ian is whispering to Dana Keller, and I can't hear what they're saying, but I read *thank you* on Ian's lips. That's when I belatedly realize exactly what's happening here.

I've been set up.

Lara's no longer desperate to get to the bathroom. Dana stuffs her untouched notebook back into her evening bag before shaking Ian's hand and then Kennedy's, who's appeared on her other side.

They planned this. How did I not see it coming? *Me*, the one who taught them everything they know about a proper setup. Damn. They did good. Really good.

But why?

Matt takes a step toward me, his smile gone, his expression shifting from playful to intense.

"What are you doing?" I whisper.

Without breaking my gaze, he reaches into his pocket. He pulls out a teal Tiffany box, flicks it open with his thumb. The ring is huge, sparkling, and perfect.

"You said you wanted a Tiffany cut, but if that was hypothetical or you've changed your mind, we'll get you a new one."

My hand goes to my heart. "What? What are you—"

Before I can finish my sentence, he calmly and unapologetically drops to one knee. "Sabrina Cross . . ."

I hear someone sob. Probably Lara. Or Kate. Maybe both.

Then I realize it's *me*. *I'm* crying.

"Don't you dare tell me it's too soon," Matt continues. "Don't tell me we've just started dating, because that's bullshit and you know it."

"Very romantic," Kennedy mutters from behind me, and I let out a little laugh, because it's so us. Only Matt's proposal would include profanity. Only his proposal to *me*.

And yet . . .

"You don't want to marry me, Matt," I whisper. "You don't believe in love."

He flicks the wrist holding the ring box in the general vicinity of the ground. "I'm kneeling on the floor in a tux, Cross. I'm pretty sure I want to get married."

Not good enough. I lift my chin defiantly, wanting it all. "Why?"

Matt smiles confidently, but before he can answer, another man in a tuxedo appears in our periphery.

"Hey, Lanham." Matt doesn't even look his way as he says it, all his attention on me.

I glance nervously toward Jarod, expecting him to be irate, but there's an almost triumphant look on his face as he takes in the scene in front of him.

"Not sure your proposing to my date is the best way to get my business," Jarod says, crossing his arms.

"I don't want your business," Matt says without hesitation.

"What?" I ask, my gaze swinging back to Matt.

Jarod says nothing.

"Kennedy will take you on." Matt says in an indifferent tone.

"Damn coin toss," I hear Ian mutter. Lara rubs his shoulder soothingly.

I shake my head in confusion. "You're giving up a multibillion-dollar account—"

"I'd give up everything for you. Every client, every last dollar."

"Matt," I whisper. "You've always wanted—"

"*You.* I've always wanted you. That much I've known for a long time, but what I didn't know until this week was that I loved you. I *love* you, Sabrina. Please, for the love of God, tell me it's not too late."

My tears are falling in earnest now. Kate sneaks forward to stuff a tissue into my hand before quickly scooting back.

I dab at my eyes, trying to clean up the worst of the mascara mess. "Will you please stand up? You look ridiculous."

He does as I ask, closing the distance between us and slipping his free hand around my back. "Say yes," he whispers in my ear. "Please say yes."

Like there was ever a choice. There's never been any choice but him.

I hold out my left hand. "Put that ring on my finger."

He lets out a little laugh, his head falling forward in relief. When his head lifts again, his eyes are darker blue and shining with unshed tears. "You still want me?" he asks roughly.

I smile and wiggle my finger.

"Sabrina." His voice is urgent now. Nearly begging.

I smile and kiss his chin. "Hell yes, I want you. I love you, Matt Cannon."

He pulls the ring out of the box, and the second he slides it onto my finger, he kisses me, hard and fast and completely unapologetic for the fact that we're basically making out in public.

I kiss him back, wonderfully aware of the weight of the ring on my finger, the applause of our friends in the background, but mostly aware of him.

"You know what I think?" he whispers, pulling back.

"Hmm?" I ask happily.

He smiles. "We're going to rock the hell out of this happily-ever-after business."

I pull his head down for another kiss. *Count on it.*

Epilogue

Sabrina

Three Months Later, January

"Four babies. Final offer."

I drop olives into my martini and add a twist to Matt's. "You do realize you're negotiating with yourself, right? I haven't issued a single counteroffer."

He comes up beside me, wrapping an arm around my waist as he lifts his cocktail. "Three babies."

I tap his chest with a fingernail. "Maybe you should wait until we've been married more than three weeks before suggesting three babies."

"Actually, I take it back," he muses. "I'm going back to four. Four kids."

I laugh. "How about enjoying cocktails as newlyweds before we skip straight to the procreation bit?"

"Deal," he says, brushing a kiss against my lips.

I wind my free arm around his back, kissing him with every ounce of besotted newlywed passion coursing through my body.

Which is a lot.

Despite my suggestion that we let Ian and Lara tie the knot first, Matt declared me too much of a flight risk.

We were married on New Year's Eve in a quiet ceremony at the place where it all began . . . sort of.

Las Vegas.

This time there were no strippers, no lurking journalists. Just close friends. Matt's parents were there as well, plus Felicia. And though Matt rolled his eyes, I don't think the atypical family showing bothered him as much as it might have a few months ago.

If we've taught each other anything, it's that we're both too stubborn and strong-willed to let other people's bad choices dictate our lives any longer.

I'd invited my mother. She hadn't come, and I was relieved. So, I wasn't blessed with a great mom. Or even a good one. It doesn't matter anymore. I have Ian. I have Lara and Kate, and even Kennedy, in his crusty old way. I have a dozen other good friends who I know I can call whenever I need anything.

Another surprise addition to our friendship circle? Jarod Lanham. He gave Matt his business after all. Turns out his whole plan to take me to the gala was a test of sorts, to assess Matt's character. At least that's his claim. Matt insists he's just trying to save his pride, but I'm not so sure. Jarod's taken to calling himself our rich, manly matchmaker, and I think he just might be right. For that matter, the whole group played the matchmaker role of sorts.

I'm grateful. I'm grateful for everyone and everything that led me to this moment. That's led me to Matt.

He's everything I need that I didn't know I wanted.

Well, *almost*.

I pull back from the kiss and smile up at him. "Two babies. Final offer. And I want to be married for at least a year."

He grins. "I'll take that offer on one condition."

I sip my drink. "What's that?"

He waggles his eyebrows and takes my drink from my hand, setting it aside. "We get lots of practice before the year is up."

"Deal," I say with a laugh, letting him scoop me up and carry me to the bedroom.

I'll be honest, I sort of want three or four babies myself. But no need to concede the game just yet.

Matt and I may be wildly in love, but we're also still *us*.

And I wouldn't have it any other way.

AUTHOR'S NOTE

Dear friends,

Thanks so much for reading *Hard Sell*! I hope you enjoyed Matt and Sabrina's book! Theirs was a special sort of love story. When I first conceived of the 21 Wall Street series, I knew that I wanted to include a "longtime enemies turned lovers" type of story. All through Book One (*Hot Asset*), I thought Matt and Sabrina were that story. And they were, in a way, but when I started writing the book, something different developed than what I'd originally intended.

They're enemies, yes, in that they bicker. And they have some messy history. But as I got to know Matt and Sabrina a bit better during the first draft, I discovered something delightful: they were also friends. Friends *and* enemies. So I let them evolve on the page *their* way, and when I finished, I realized that I didn't quite have the enemies-to-lovers story I'd originally envisioned. It was more of a frenemies-to-lovers story, which I think made it all the more special because their relationship was so unique and layered. I so hope you agree!

If you're new to the 21 Wall Street series, be sure to check out *Hot Asset,* which is Ian and Lara's story. (A female SEC agent falling for the playboy suspect in a career-making insider-trading case? Heck yes!)

As for Kennedy and Kate's story . . . I can't say. I don't know yet. But I assure you, my fingers are crossed.

In the meantime, be sure to check out my website (www.laurenlayne.com) for a full list of my books!

Happy reading,

Lauren Layne

ACKNOWLEDGMENTS

Thank you so much to my agent, Nicole Resciniti, who immediately, and without hesitation, got behind my vision of writing "hot Wall Street guys" and found the perfect home for it at Montlake Romance.

I couldn't be more grateful for the Montlake team, especially Maria Gomez, my fabulous editor, who's an absolute delight to work with. To the cover design and marketing team, who blow me away with their vision and enthusiasm. To the production team and operation teams, who work tirelessly behind the scenes to turn a messy document into a flawless final product.

And most especially, thank you to Kristi Yanta, my developmental editor, who I so often refer to as my "brain twin," because she always understands what I'm trying to do, and quite often knows how to do it *better* than I ever imagine. I'm forever honored to have a place on your client list. I'm grateful to call you a friend as well as my editor and so appreciate that you're always there for me whenever I need you (which, let's face it . . . is often).

Lastly, thank you to Lisa Filipe, my friends, family, and all my lovely readers. I don't thank you all nearly enough for the quiet support that's so very much appreciated.

ABOUT THE AUTHOR

Photo © 2016 Anthony LeDonne

Lauren Layne is the *New York Times* bestselling author of more than two dozen romantic comedies, including *Hot Asset*, her first book in the 21 Wall Street series. A former e-commerce and web marketing manager from Seattle, Lauren relocated to New York City to pursue a full-time writing career, hitting the *USA Today*, *New York Times*, iBooks, and Amazon bestseller lists. Visit the author at www.laurenlayne.com.